Horror in the Night
The Secrets of Whispering Willows

Book 1

Gregory's Story

By: Mary Reason Theriot

Dedication

Without the love and support of my family and friends, I would not have pursued this new path in life. I would especially like to thank those that have proofread copy after copy, to give me their honest opinion of the books.

Theresa, thank you so much for your continued encouragement. Without you, some of the characters would not have "come to life."

To my wonderful husband Malwen, your continued love and support mean the world to me. I do not know what I would do without you in my life. One of these nights I am sure you will be able to sleep with both eyes closed. Eventually, I should run out of ideas... or maybe not. These books would not be what they are without you pushing me forward.

To Yuri Theriot and Don Reason for your input.

To Don Reason and Malcolm "Phil" Theriot for sharing your knowledge and experience of Law Enforcement protocol.

To my fans, I would like to offer a special thank you for your continued support.

I would also like to thank Louis Dupuy for his amazing work on the book cover.

ISBN-10: 1-945393-04-1
ISBN-13: 978-1-945393-04-4

Also Available by Mary Reason Theriot

The Hideaway

The Traveler

Dr. Frankenstein

Above Suspicion

www.maryreasontheriot.com

Prologue

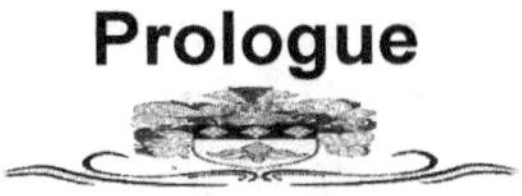

He made his money from killing. Sometimes he killed
animals, but mainly he enjoyed killing people. He was good
at what he did - maybe one of the best in his field. This was
not his ego talking, but the honest truth. Of course, the
military helped him hone his skills. While in the military,
he'd learned how to come and go like a ghost in the night.

He preferred to find victims in the bigger cities, where
people lived cheek to cheek and no one cared about those
around them. No one wanted to get involved. When you
walked down the street no one bothered to make eye
contact or say hello. In the bigger cities, the sheer number
and variety of victims astounded him. It was a veritable
buffet for him. The trick was not getting too greedy, to
switch cities. That allowed him to take his time and choose
with care. If they had an offensive smell, he moved on. He
didn't need to stink up the trunk of his car with something
that reminded him of rotting cabbage.

Gregory Ferris had been killing for years. Creeping about
town at night, lurking in the shadows. Darkness suited him;
it was filled with mystery. The unknown had always
intrigued him. He could move around , letting the stars
navigate his way with their pinpricks of light. He had
learned how to be cautious. His career had been successful
due to his caution in all aspects of life.

Even after displaying the bodies for the world to see, he had
yet to be discovered. The public and media referred to him

as the "master of horror," speculating on how he got his Halloween props to look so life-like.

With each prop, he let his imagination run wild. There were various ways to pose a body that would shock and degrade most individuals. However, when he added them as an attraction to his haunted house for Halloween, the masses couldn't get enough. It thrilled him to know that he could kill with complete anonymity, yet display his works of art for the world to see.

He enjoyed taking the time to watch people. It had become a very enlightening hobby. Observing various human behaviors was an adventure. It was also an integral part of his work. Just from their mannerisms, sometimes he could envision how they should look in a particular scene. He had been known to design a scene around one perfect model.

This business had also taught him patience. Timing was crucial when he abducted a subject. If he discovered a person perfect for a particular idea, he waited for the opportune moment to capture that person. If he realized they were not what he needed, then he moved on. If they didn't deserve to become an integral part of the haunted house, he didn't allow them the privilege to join. Only those that met his criteria were chosen.

He loved looking at a person and fantasizing about the different scenarios in which he could use them in the haunted house. The possibilities could be endless if the right person caught his fancy.

He was ready to begin another creation. He anxiously waited for the rush that was about to come. His skin tingled from head to toe as the euphoria of the moment took over his body. His first attempts at prop making were amateurish. He'd tried to make his props from foam and other materials, but he could never achieve the look he wanted.

Over the years, he had perfected his avocation, learning to be innovative with his prop making. He had found that ordinary beeswax worked best when mixed with a secret chemical compound that hardened the material and increased its resistance to extreme temperature. To produce the amount of wax he needed, he had his own bee hives so he could have a steady supply. This wax had a slight translucent consistency when poured over the bodies. The beeswax concoction was applied over the human flesh as the final layer. It also helped to preserve the body, thus accounting for his Halloween props having an uncanny similarity to an actual human being. What made him so superb at his particular avocation was that he had no empathy towards people. He treated each of his subjects as works of art.

The best subjects for him to use were prostitutes, the homeless and runaways; people that law enforcement agencies considered high-risk victims. He needed to be certain that he did not have someone searching for a loved one after they disappeared. It would not do to display a work of art and then have that person recognized.

Chapter 1

Point Creole, Louisiana

Point Creole, Louisiana was a small Cajun town located along Bayou Teche in Southeast Louisiana. Until now, there had always been a sense of peacefulness that made people feel safe and secure. But could one ever feel truly safe?

The citizens of Point Creole were proud of their heritage. Several of the original buildings and plantation homes dating back two centuries remained intact. It felt as if you were stepping back in time when you entered some of the antique stores and businesses.

Point Creole was near several larger cities, which brought in tourists to the idyllic little town. Several Creole restaurants and plantations offered tours to keep the tourists coming. There was a relaxed, unhurried feel about the town.

It was also the perfect place for him to set up his next house of horrors. Gregory Ferris was known for his haunted houses across the south. For several years he had made a living out of scaring people, having them flee from the building like frightened children. Scaring people was a lucrative business. Every year people returned in droves to see how they would be scared. He was ready to set up another house of fright, and he believed Point Creole would be an excellent location.

Two rows of ancient oak trees framed the plantation home that caught his interest. Walking through the old oak trees would help set the mood. The branches resembled grotesque arms reaching out to grab those that dared to enter the house. Gnarled roots reached up from the ground as if bodies were making their way out of unmarked graves. Even though he didn't believe in haunted houses, just looking at this house sent a chill down his spine. Yes, he had chosen the perfect place. Just looking at the old plantation home sent your heart racing in fear.

He'd found the place by accident and it had piqued his interest. He could set everything up without fear of curious bystanders. The locals believed the area was haunted and even warned him not to purchase the place. They thought fear and mystery surrounded the house.

He was proud of his success. His current haunted house had been a success for several years now. He had improved on it each year. Critics had always said his scenes looked realistic and wondered how he did it. If they knew they were in an actual house of horrors, would his attractions still be as popular?

It was as if something unearthly drew him to this place, past the maze of bayous and roads. One look at the old plantation home and he knew it was what he had been searching for. It would be perfect for what he had planned. This may be the best attraction he had opened yet. It offered many rooms where he could create several scenarios for the Haunted Plantation. The sheer size of the house rendered it terrifying. The dark, dilapidated corridors, old rusted pipes and flaking paint enhanced the haunted look.

Before venturing closer to the house, he had to watch his step. The terrain was treacherous and unpredictable. For the safety of the paying guests coming to visit the haunted house, he needed to make sure the walkway was clearly lit.

Walking through this house, he realized it was the epitome of what he wanted. The house seemed to have an essence about it, as though it was engulfed in evil. Just walking up to the house gave you an eerie feeling. He needed to add a lazy iron gate to the property to give the yard an even more haunted appearance. Towards the bayou, he envisioned an old cemetery with aging headstones greeting guests.

This monstrous house had a Greek inspired architecture. It stood over three stories tall, and it was rumored to have a basement. It had a wide wraparound porch with French doors that led into the house. The black shutters framing the windows desperately needed a painting. However, it looked as if all of the shutters were still here, albeit haphazardly. There appeared to be rotten wood around a good bit of the exterior that needed repairing. He needed to ascertain what had to be repaired structurally, and leave everything else as is.

When he stepped into the house, he felt as if he had stepped back in time. Cobwebs and dust covered most of the interior surfaces, which helped accentuate the haunted atmosphere.

The hardwood floors had lost their luster, but he could tell how grand this house must have been at one time. In the foyer, various pictures and pieces of furniture were strewn about. The house still boasted golden, gilt-edged wainscoting, velvet wallpaper, crystal chandeliers, and ornate furniture. Antique dealers would be thrilled to get their hands on the wondrous possessions left behind. He planned to use as much of this as possible for the haunted house.

In the center of the foyer was a grand staircase that needed to be checked for stability. A crystal chandelier still hung from the ceiling, which once welcomed guests into the brilliance of the house. The foyer would be the ideal place to start the tour, before continuing through the maze of rooms.

To the left was a formal parlor. It had a massive fireplace with a finely carved mantle, as well as intricate woodwork around the room. To the right of the foyer was a grand dining room. In it sat a table that showed its age. It was almost as if the previous owners stepped away from the house, intent on coming back, but never did. He needed to research the history of the plantation to incorporate it into the tour.

He did learn from the locals that at one time, this had been a flourishing plantation. Slaves toiled in the fields, growing and picking cotton and sugarcane. The crops were loaded onto barges, making their way through the bayous, and eventually to the city of New Orleans, where the cargo was then sold.

At one time, the family who owned this property had been wealthy and influential. He wondered why the plantation had been abandoned.

Before beginning work on the haunted house, he posted no trespassing signs to keep out any unwanted hunters and the like. He had had problems with people honoring the signs at the other location, but the realtor stressed that in this area of Louisiana, they respected your privacy and obeyed the signs. He noticed several of the same signs posted nearby, so he hoped this was true. He would set up some motion-activated cameras to make certain. In the beginning, he would often be gone while he made the necessary preparations. He needed new subjects for his props, and he needed to get started as soon as possible.

For the first few days, he checked the cameras frequently, to ensure that no locals had become curious. So far, he had been lucky, and had had no visitors. After purchasing the home, he also bought several large freezers to store body parts. The old refrigerator would be used to hold blood. The bodies would not keep until Halloween before decomposition set in, so he needed to embalm them before preparing the props. He was still learning how to preserve some of his favorite pieces. Even after embalming they decomposed, but at a slower pace. He was still perfecting his embalming and preservation techniques.

He tried to have an equal mix of men and women. After all, he needed diversity. He would also attempt several new wax features. He needed to install a commercial air conditioner to keep the old home at the ideal temperature while the haunted house was being built, and while it was open to the public.

It was now November, which gave him less than a year to have everything prepared. Thankfully, he had started searching for the next location ahead of time. Everything was ready for him to begin. Next year he would have both locations open, and each would be a great success if everything went well. He needed everything completed and ready for the grand opening the first weekend of October.

Chapter 2

It was a humid night on the river. The moon was only a sly smile in the sky. From the moment he stepped outside, he felt the charge in the air. Tonight he would find the perfect creation for his vision. He preferred not to hunt this close to home, but something in the air empowered him. He had learned not to ignore this feeling when it came over him. If the opportunity reared its wondrous head, in whatever form it may take, he would act upon it.

***

Though it was almost daybreak, Sandy Bryant was not ready to go home. She had no one to go home to, no one to love her. She was all alone. She still couldn't believe the bartender kicked her out; telling her she'd had too much to drink. Who did he think he was? She had money and she could pay her tab for a change.

The humid air had her skin slick with sweat. The dank smell of the bayou filled the air. It was eerily quiet; even the crickets were silent tonight. There was no traffic on the road. She needed to find another bar that was open. She wanted to forget about her problems.

Up ahead, she thought she heard footsteps. Maybe she would run into someone who wanted to have a good time with her. She didn't care to party by herself. She peered into the night, trying to see what made the noise. For a moment, she swore something evil was looming out there in the darkness, waiting for her.

Suddenly scared, her blood ran cold. She searched the shadows, trying to see if someone, or something, was out there. Then she saw it, not far behind her, a dark figure. It was as if it was watching and waiting. The fine hairs on her forearms rose. It had to be her imagination. Besides, she did have a lot to drink tonight. There was nothing threatening out here. She looked around once more and the shadow had disappeared. It was just her imagination.

Then her skin began to crawl and her paranoia went into overdrive. Someone was watching her.

"Stop being silly," she chided herself.

The hazy blue light cast by the street lights ahead helped illuminate her way as she staggered off in search of another bar. She didn't want to stay around to find out who may be lurking in the shadows.

***

He was about to give up, thinking his intuition had been wrong about tonight, when he saw her. She was stumbling down the street, highly intoxicated, right past the French Quarter. She was exactly what he had been looking for, an incredibly sexy body, but a face only a mother could love. Her outfit looked as if she had just come off her night job. She wore a tight mini skirt, a tube top that barely covered her full breasts, and stilettos that must be impossible to walk in considering the inebriated state she was in tonight.

He must not have been as quiet as he thought because she turned around suddenly and ran into him. She tried to right herself.

Acting quickly, he placed the ether soaked rag over her mouth and nostrils. She was too drunk to put up a fight. He "assisted" her back to his car. With the stench of alcohol that surrounded her, any passerby would not think twice about him "escorting" her.

***

Once he had her on the table at the plantation, he observed her body better. Battle scars were evident from her life on the streets. From the looks of her nose, she had broken it numerous times along with several other bones. From the way they protruded from her body, even to the naked eye, it was evident she'd never had them set by a doctor.

The table was one he had designed especially for this process. It was a stainless steel table made from a grated material. After he had finished with his prop making, he needed to insert them directly into the beeswax. With the contraptions he'd installed, he could roll the table over to the vat of hot beeswax and lower his creations into it. Once coated, he could carefully lift them and let the beeswax drip off.

The various work stations around the room allowed him to work on several props at once without tying up his equipment.

Looking at her nose gave him an idea. He brought his chair closer to the unconscious body and began his work.

He picked up a hammer and swung at her face, breaking her nose. He then proceeded to flail away at various other areas of her body. The pain woke her. Her animalistic screams shattered the silence of the night.

He stared down at the terrified young girl; pain etched across her face. Her face twisted in an ugly fashion as she let out another guttural scream. She tried to beg him to stop, but blood gurgled in her mouth.

As he picked up a hammer and prepared to hit her body once again, she gurgled out, "Please stop. Why are you doing this?"

He didn't bother to acknowledge the fact that she was speaking. As she continued to glare at him, he heard a voice in his head saying she needed to be killed now, but he wasn't satisfied with the look of her body. It must be perfect.

Ferris positioned a stool in front of her and pulled out his knife. With slow deliberation, he moved the knife along the stone. Her eyes were wide with fear as she noticed each pass the blade made along the stone. Once finished, he ran it along the skin of his arm and watched as it shaved off a fine layer of hair. A smile of satisfaction formed across his face. "Perfect, don't you think? It should be sharp enough now."

"For what?" She asked as her eyes glistened with fresh tears.

He rose to his feet to move the stool and explained, "For me to complete my work."

***

Oh dear Lord, what did this man have planned? Her mind raced with images of the vicious, vile things he could do to her. Fear reignited her attempt to escape. She struggled against the restraints. A dozen promises and resolutions ran off her lips as she bartered with God to save her. She vowed to change her ways and go on the straight and narrow if she lived.

Why was this happening to her? The pain was like nothing she had ever experienced.   Why didn't he just let her die?

She had lost so much blood,that it seemed to cover the room. She should be dead. There was no escape; no one would come to her rescue. Death couldn't come quickly enough. Stab wounds riddled her body, but none deep enough to kill her. Her tormentor was relentless, only cutting her shallow enough to draw blood and cause her pain. So far, no wounds had been near fatal enough to let death take her away from this place. She could feel the stickiness of the blood on her skin, smell its coppery scent. If only she could block the blood out of her mind and not think of the pain.

She felt him press the syringe to her neck. Her lungs were instantly on fire. She felt the strength leaving her body as blackness began enveloping her.

***

He found the process fascinating as he let his creative juices flow. He had yet to feel remorse for killing anyone for his artwork. Besides, none of these people had much of a life.

Life had been cruel to them, and they were better off dead. He was doing them and the world a favor.

Once he had performed enough torture on her body, he injected her with the CO2 cartridge, killing her quickly.

Looking at the mangled body, he realized that it was perfect. It would be the piece de resistance for the torture chamber. Now that he was finished, he needed to get the body covered with the beeswax so that he could keep it looking fresh. He didn't want decomp to set in and change the color of the body. Acting fast, he began the tedious process.

While bringing the prop to the basement, he stopped to adjust one of the heads on the banister. He took a moment to look at it, pleased with the results. There were two heads applied to the banister, their lifeless eyes welcoming those that dared to go upstairs. Two more heads were at the top of the staircase. He was currently replacing the spindles on the stairs with various arms and legs. It was a time consuming process. Each arm and leg needed to have the bones removed, and a spindle inserted into the limb. It was then sewn back up and placed on the stairs. The gruesome staircase was constructed with the random placement of limbs.

He looked up to see if his winged man remained secured safely in the rafters. This ingenious idea came to him one night as he watched an owl swoop down on a field mouse. From up above, this winged creature would swoop down onto the crowd, circle the area, and retreat to his hiding place before he did it again for the next group. The creature he had created was a man's body with four legs and two wings. Instead of feathers for the wings, though, there was skin stretched tight with bones showing.

He had also made another winged creature for the upstairs. That one reminded him of a giant moth. The creature, gray in color, stood over seven feet tall, had large red eyes, and a pair of monstrous wings that spanned approximately seven feet across.

He used the gory leftover torsos as well. He was working on adding robotics to several of them. He hoped to have the torsos crawling along on the floor of the torture room. There was so much to accomplish that he hoped he had it finished in time.

Chapter 3

Eric Davis walked into the night with nothing to illuminate the sidewalks but the dim streetlights. Doorways cloaked in shadows could hide even the vilest of souls. While accustomed to walking these streets at this hour, a feeling of trepidation raised the hairs on the back of his neck. Goose bumps formed on his skin.

A light breeze blew through the trees, ruffling the leaves. The slight sound sent a chill racing down his spine. A cold certainty washed over him - he was being watched. His gut clenched as he looked around. Seeing nothing, he continued walking.

A flicker of movement in the shadows startled him. Something in the alley moved. A shadow darted to the other side. His heart beat wildly against his chest.

He picked up his pace and rushed back to the little motel room he used as his apartment. He still hadn't told his parents where he was. He had to leave that small town where people judged you for what you had and not who you were. Those sanctimonious bastards wouldn't give him a break when he came out of the closet and let everyone know he was gay. They acted as if he had committed a cardinal sin. Knowing he would never have a life there, he packed up and left in the middle of the night. He found a job for an airline company and had been a steward for the last several months. It was a fantastic job, and the people treated him with respect.

Goosebumps spread over his body when he heard footsteps approaching from behind him. He never knew what hit him. Before he could even turn, he felt a sudden jolt of electricity course through his body. He fell to the ground.

***

The night was ending. The moon hung low on the horizon. It wouldn't be long before the sun's first rays kissed the morning sky. It had been a lengthy drive to Point Creole. Gregory was anxious to return to the plantation and begin putting together the next prop. Exhilaration was what had kept him up all night. Besides, he wouldn't be able to sleep until he completed the project.

He pulled into the overgrown drive that led to the plantation. Once he stopped the car, he got out and slammed the car door with his hip. The crickets incessant chirping welcomed him back home. He heard a rustle near the bayou, more than likely an alligator on the prowl for something to eat. He looked out at the bayou, the morning sky was a blaze of pinks turning a fiery orange as the sun crept into view.

He walked to the back of the car and popped open the trunk. His newest subject was still unconscious. Acting quickly, he brought the young man inside and secured him to the operating table. It took skill to do what he was about to do. He'd retrofitted the room with every possible gadget he needed to make his props.

***

Eric slowly woke up. It was hard to clear the fog from his brain. When he went to sit up, panic gripped his body. He couldn't move his legs or arms. They seemed to be strapped down to a table of some sort. He could feel the cold steel against his naked back.

Panicked thoughts ran through his brain. Where was he? What was going on? He tried to concentrate, attempting to recall what he'd done last night. He attempted to pull free of his bindings, but the effort was futile. He took in a deep breath, trying to force himself to relax when the smell hit him. It was unlike anything he had ever encountered before. As if food was rotting nearby.

He heard footsteps approaching. Someone was coming. What if it was his abductor ? How could he protect himself?

A man appeared before him and studied him intently. "I'm so glad you are finally awake. I have such big plans for you. Before I begin, I just want you to know how important of a role you will be playing."

Eric's mind was reeling. A role ? What kind of role ? Was this a snuff film? He had heard about people being forced to participate against their will.

"Don't worry; I'm quite skilled at this, and you are perfect for what I have in mind." When the man stood up, Eric noticed the meat hooks dangling from the ceiling. "Oh, don't worry; I have no plans to use those on you."

***

Ferris wheeled the cart holding his surgical instruments closer. Selecting a scalpel, he turned to face his victim. The young man trembled as the shiny blade made contact with his neck. Blood oozed from the shallow cut. He heard the man take in a deep breath from the sting of the wound. The smell of blood filled the room.

"Why are you doing this to me?"

Ferris smiled down at the young man, "This is all for entertainment. You will be part of a famous haunted house that will be talked about for years to come."

Once satisfied with his work, he picked up the CO2 cartridge and released the young man from the pain. Looking down at the body, he was pleased with his knife work. Several gaping wounds revealed bone. He spread apart the wounds, so that tendon could be seen. This young man would become one of his zombies, but for that to work he had to let the body decay so that he achieved the correct pigmentation. He was elated to see that he'd captured the look of terror and pain on the subject's face as he died. He couldn't have planned it better.

He forced the dead man's mouth open. After he drained the body of blood, he would remove the teeth. It would be a long and arduous process, but the teeth needed to be removed so that he could file them down to sharp points. Soon the lips should retreat, almost disappearing, giving Ferris the look he desired for this prop.

The basement level would be a torture chamber, and it must be perfect. There would be zombies and tortured souls trying to escape.

He set up several fog machines and misters, to give his guests the feeling they were walking through a damp portal and straight into the bowels of hell.

When he'd planned his first haunted house, he reined in his imagination, but with this one he was stopping at nothing. He planned to have a creature at the bottom of the stairs that would appear to be spitting out "acid" as people came near. He also had a zombie that was gorging itself on brains near the middle of the room. He would use several of his victims to display in the torture chamber. There were black lights to illuminate the creatures. He mixed the beeswax with a special chemical that fluoresced under black light just for these props. The black light gave them an eerie appearance and a life-like aura. He was especially proud of this addition.

Now that the pneumatics were working properly, the torsos could roam through the basement, creeping along the dirt floor. A few of the underground graves had skeletons and zombies that jumped out. It would be an eerie experience when guests walked through the basement to exit into the graveyard. He had added a few lurches in the mix as well. Just when guests believed they were free of the crawling zombies, one would jump out at them, almost as if it was trying to grab them and drag them in with him.

After exiting the basement, visitors entered the graveyard on the side of the house. There would be a gravedigger and more zombies. The gravestones had had the fluorescent chemical splattered on them as well. There were also several skeletons displayed sporadically throughout the graveyard. Through the fog and darkness, visitors had to navigate their way past the skeletons, zombies, and headstones in order to exit the haunted house.

The black lights not only helped light the way, but also gave it the ambiance he wanted. Every time he closed his eyes, he could envision the screams that would emit from the crowds of people that would come through here.

Due to all the pneumatics, he'd had to add another breaker box to handle the extra electrical load. If everything went well, this would be an experience none of his guests forgot.

Chapter 4

As Gregory drove to New Orleans to pick up more supplies, he felt his phone vibrate before it had a chance to ring. It was his best friend, Thomas Billiot. Gregory and Thomas had been friends since kindergarten. He had been so busy, though, that Gregory hadn't checked in with Thomas. "Mon ami, what's up?"

"I was wondering if you are in town today and can meet me for lunch."

"As a matter of fact, I am. How about Frenchie's at 1:00 p.m.?" He wondered what Thomas had on his mind. He rarely called unexpectedly for lunch.

It was a few minutes before one o'clock when Gregory arrived at the restaurant. The place was still extremely busy. Almost all of the booths and tables were occupied. Conversation was buzzing through the room as he peered around to see if his best friend had made it there before him. So far, he hadn't seen him though.

A hostess finally appeared, "I'm meeting a friend of mine, Thomas Billiot, for lunch. Has he made it yet?"

"No, sir, not that I know of but let me show you to a table."

As the hostess led him to the table, he looked around. It was one of their favorite places to eat when they got together for lunch. It was a down home creole restaurant, nothing fancy, that served excellent food.

As Gregory settled in, Thomas arrived. Standing up, he shook his best friend's hand. "What's up with the lunch invite?"

"I needed a break from my stuffy office and wanted to check on you, make sure you aren't killing yourself while preparing for the newest haunted house. How is it coming by the way?"

"It is slow, but coming along. I'm letting my imagination run wild with this one. Actually, I'm having a hard time restraining myself and want to add more and more. I need to pace myself, or I won't be able to finish."

"I wish you would let me hire you some help. At least a couple of young guys you can order around and let them do the grunt work. You are going to work yourself into an early grave if you don't watch it."

"I won't be able to trust anyone else to do the job. We both know I have control problems. I would spend more time going behind someone and making sure they were doing it right, or just end up doing it myself anyhow."

"I just want you to take it easy, my friend, that's all."

The waitress stopped by to take their orders. Thomas ordered a bowl of gumbo while Gregory had an envie, a craving, for a shrimp po'boy and French fries.

As he enjoyed his po'boy, Thomas stated, "At least you still have an appetite."

Gregory drug a French fry through some ketchup before stuffing it in his mouth, "I've been so busy that I usually warm up something quick and get back to work. This really hits the spot." After popping another fry in his mouth, "I may have to order another plate to go just so I can make sure I eat tonight."

"You work too hard."

Gregory looked up at him in astonishment, "That may be, but it will be a spectacular grand opening day if all goes well. I can already hear the screams and see them running in fear from the haunted house."

Thomas laughed, "I have no doubt that it will be a huge success."

As they finished their meal, Gregory saw a remarkable young woman walk into the restaurant. Thomas noticed him looking, "That's the new voodoo shop owner. She's a looker isn't she?"

"She sure is." Looking at the way she moved and carried herself gave him an idea. He needed to dedicate a section to voodoo. Voodoo was big in New Orleans. The voodoo practiced here originated from the traditions of the African diaspora. It developed here in Louisiana among the French, Spanish, and Creole speaking African American population of the state. Louisiana Voodoo was often confused with Haitian Voodoo, but there were some differences.

Marie Fourchet walked past their table, her colorful dress billowing around her. As if in a trance, he watched her. Oh yes, he had to find a woman that resembled her. He could already imagine how the room would look.

Chapter 5

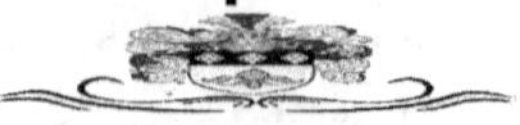

Mardi Gras was a popular celebration in Louisiana. King Cakes went on sale before families finished celebrating Christmas. Mardi Gras was now in full swing across the state.

The local Krewes were having their Mardi Gras balls and parades. Everyone dressed in lavish costumes for the events. But Gregory could live without Mardi Gras this year. However, if he did not make an appearance, the public would become curious as to why he suddenly became antisocial.

As he dressed for the ball, he decided he would make his appearance and leave. As crowded as these parties were, no one would notice that he'd left early. Most people would be too drunk to notice him missing.

The town was inundated with tourists that allowed him the perfect opportunity to search for new subjects. He may as well make his time away from the haunted house useful, especially if he wanted to make progress.

***

Amy Guillory ordered herself one more daiquiri before heading home. She had promised her friends that she would celebrate Mardi Gras with them, but her heart wasn't in it. She still couldn't believe Shawn Granger was such a loser. He would rather sit in front of the TV and play video games instead of going out and having some real fun with her. Seriously, what was it with these guys and their video games? Would she ever hook up with a real man? Someone who could hold a job?

Mad at the world, Amy stomped out of the bar and headed down Front Street, hoping to blow off some steam and alcohol.

It was harder than she expected to walk in these damn high heels, especially when she was wasted. When she bent down to remove her heels, she thought she heard someone walk up behind her. She looked up and saw a man wearing a mask. Her grandmother's warning reverberated through her mind, *"Be wary of strangers cher. Don't trust anyone."* She pushed that thought aside; maybe he was what she needed to forget about Shawn.

Before she knew it, strong arms grabbed her, holding her tight. She attempted to push him away, but it was of no use. Before she could scream, he covered her nose and mouth with an ether soaked rag. She tried not to breathe in the cloyingly sweet drug, but his grasp was too powerful. She slumped heavily in his arms

She had a hard time opening her eyes. When she did open her eyes, it was nearly impossible to focus on anything around her. Nothing looked familiar. "Where am I?" she asked aloud.

"Shh, you are all right cher. The moment I saw you I knew you had to be included in my haunted house. Your bone structure is sheer perfection."

She tried to move her head back and forth, hoping to shake the fog out of her brain. She couldn't understand what he was saying.

A sense of dread washed over her. She attempted to sit up, but soon realized that she was strapped to a table of some kind. She tried to break free, but the restraints were too tight.

"Please don't hurt me. I'll do whatever you want me to, I swear," her voice quaked with fear as she spoke. As her captor began his torture, the pain became unrelenting.

***

Once satisfied with his work, he injected her neck with the CO_2 cartridge. He watched as the life faded from her eyes. He wheeled the body over to a vat of beeswax to prepare her for her final preparations.

The props were coming together for the various scenes.

Chapter 6

As he stepped into the night, his eyes focused through the darkness. He breathed in the dark, insidious aroma of the Mississippi River. The scents and the breeze across his face reminded him he was home again. He had been hunting here more than he should, but he doubted anyone would miss those he had chosen.

Jamie DuPont stood on the street corner and stared out into the night. Even though Gregory was engulfed in the darkness of the night, he swore that she was looking directly at him. His black, glittering eyes watched her every movement. A feral hunger moved through him. She was perfect for a prop he had been longing to do. She reminded him of a voodoo priestess. Her caramel skin was sheer perfection and her mesmerizing eyes drew you in.

***

Jamie stomped her feet on the sidewalk trying to get the blood flowing again in her body. It was bitterly cold out tonight. She'd thought winter was over with, but a chill stayed in the night air. It didn't help that she was dressed in her usual attire; hardly any skin was covered. She tried crossing her arms under her breasts and tucking her hands underneath. She shivered against the night air. The temperature must be keeping everyone inside. She had not seen a potential customer for almost an hour. Rent was due soon. She needed to make some money and hoped it picked up, or she would be living on the streets. At least until she could earn enough money for another roof over her head.

As the wind cut into her, she considered calling it a night. If the weather was like this tomorrow night, she might have to wear a jacket when no one was around.

For a moment, she swore she felt the presence of evil lurking about as if beckoning her into the shadows of the night. A deep, primitive fear washed over her body. She tried to shake off the eerie sensation.

***

Making sure no one was around, he walked up behind her and wrapped his powerful arms around her. She attempted to fight him off, but he was too strong. He placed the ether soaked rag over her mouth and nose and forced her to breathe in the drug. She went limp in a matter of seconds. He drug her to his car, acting as if she'd had too much to drink and needed assistance. When he arrived at his car, he looked around and locked her in the trunk.

Once he was back at the plantation, he strapped his still sleeping victim onto the table in his workroom. He had often wondered what happened when you died in your sleep, while so vulnerable and weak. What would it be like to slit their throats while they slept? Would their nightmare go on forever or would they just simply disappear into the blackness? Have those that he had killed in the past kept reliving their last moment here on earth? No, he couldn't deviate from his plans. For him to achieve what he needed; he couldn't simply cut her throat. He needed the fear to show on their faces, and that was not something he could manually manipulate. It had to come from the heart.

***

She slowly awoke. Where was she? She had a difficult time seeing anything. Everything was one big blur. She attempted to sit up, but her arms and legs appeared to be restrained to a table. The air was cool and damp against her skin. What was happening? Why was she restrained and naked?

She tried desperately to free herself from the straps. Her efforts were futile though. She heard footsteps and, possibly, someone pushing a cart. Her heart sank. If her captor was here, then that meant there was no way to escape.

When he started torturing her, she swore the pain came at her from every direction. She writhed in agony .

***

Once satisfied with his work, he injected her neck with the CO2 cartridge. After the life had left her eyes, he wheeled the body over to a vat of beeswax to prepare her for her final stage. She was perfect for the voodoo priestess. He had already begun to set up the scene.

He'd previously prepared a six-foot boa constrictor that would be draped over her neck. He had killed it when the forked tongue was moving out of its mouth. He had visited a voodoo shop in New Orleans and bought several voodoo dolls to use in the room. He wanted his customers to feel as if they were stepping into a voodoo priestess's domicile. He had arranged a wooden altar and brought in several cypress stumps. Large oak tree limbs were suspended from the ceiling and draped with dangling Spanish moss. When people stepped into this room, they'd feel as if they were deep in the swamp. When the low-lying fog machine turned on, it gave it just the effect he wanted.

He also had captured several alligators around the property. He was glad he'd taken a course in taxidermy years ago. It was coming in handy. He had found several pairs of red glowing eyes on the internet a while back and purchased everything the company had. When he replaced the alligators' eyes with them, the outcome turned out better than he had hoped. The eyes glowed in the dark and looked positively eerie in the fog.

He had even purchased a set of voodoo drums and found a soundtrack of voodoo music that would play in the background. When the drum music started up, the sinister tone of the drums snaked and twisted throughout the house until your senses throbbed with the beat.

Beside each drum stood "small" men a little less than four feet tall. He'd had a difficult time finding four young men for these props.

The drummers had short stumpy legs, long, monkey like arms, almost flat, concave faces, large protruding eyes and elongated teeth with sinister smiles. They were covered in short, stiff hair that he removed from several nutria rats he had captured. Instead of fingernails, they had long sharp claws. These creatures would give people pause. He could envision people staring at them, trying to determine what they were. He arranged them where they appeared to be playing the drums. Their large bulging eyes glowed red thanks to the contact lenses he'd purchased. The wax helped hold them in place.

In the center of the room was the wooden voodoo altar; complete with the candles, salt bowl, skeleton and other voodoo artifacts he'd picked up from his trip to New Orleans. The voodoo priestess was the main attraction. She drew you into the room with her eyes.

He also set up an ancient torture room. He would have one girl attached to the wheel of torture. The large wheel would have numerous spikes tearing into her back as it turned. He would have a man set up near the front, controlling the wheel with a menacing sneer on his face. He could already imagine how it would look.

He'd also created another spectacular prop for this chamber. It was a man shackled to a tree with a small incision in his gut; his intestines draped outside of his body and small animals feasted on the delicacy. He'd somehow captured his face in pure visceral terror. Finding the trees for the props had been easy. After each heavy storm that struck the area, he went for a walk. He brought them in and set them up, which saved him from spending money on the props. It also helped give the haunted house an authentic look.

Chapter 7

Sienna paced restlessly in the dark alley, her steps hurried and anxious as the meth surged through her system. One hand held a lit cigarette, which she moved to and from her lips with a shaky arm while the other moved through the air in various patterns. Her mouth moved rapidly as she talked to the different personalities living in her head.

Her black fishnet stockings were torn in various places and were barely held together. She wore a well-worn black leather miniskirt, and a tight silver tank top that displayed her voluptuous breasts. Her long black hair was clumped and matted as if it hadn't been washed in days. Her face was caked heavily with makeup in an attempt to hide her age.

She should be working her corner, but was too high to care. When she came down from her current high, she would return to work. Besides, she needed this high. The voices were controlling her actions more and more. She could no longer run from them as she had in the past.

She stopped talking to herself for a moment. She thought she'd heard a noise. The gentle rustle of footsteps, possibly? Peering deep into the alley, she did not see anything, so she went back to her one sided conversation. She accidentally dropped her cigarette and squatted down to find it. The movement caused her skirt to ride up, showing off her bare backside.

An arm grabbed her from behind and another arm wrapped around her face, pressing an ether soaked rag over her nose and mouth. She tried to squeal in shock, but the rag muffled any noise she could make. She inhaled the cloyingly sweet drug and fell into a deep abyss.

Sienna awoke some time later, unaware of how long she had been unconscious. She blinked several times, allowing her eyes to adjust to her surroundings. The first thing she noticed was that she was restrained to a table of some kind. She tried to break free of the restraints, but they refused to budge.

She considered screaming, but feared that if she did, her captor would then know that she was awake. She wanted to put off the inevitable for as long as possible. Besides, it might buy her some time to figure out a way to escape. If only she could free herself from these restraints. She could hear hammering and sawing in the distance and the air had a heady smell of decay, as if something was rotting nearby.

When she heard the noise stop, she listened as footsteps approached. A large man appeared before her. He was a big man, well over six feet tall, with arms and legs corded with muscles. While his face was quite handsome, when she looked deeper into his eyes, she saw the madness dance across his face. She would never have suspected that someone who looked like him could be a demented monster. His eyes twinkled with malice.

She saw the knife in his hand and swallowed back the fear. "I'm glad you are awake. I meant to start preparations before you had woken up, but I needed to finish the room you will be exhibited in. You see, I am a bit of a perfectionist. Some of my friends say that I have obsessive compulsive tendencies."

She had a hard time imagining this man as a crazed maniac. His voice was almost soothing, as if he was trying to put her at ease.

When she felt the knife glide across her body, fear coursed through her as she waited for the pain to hit. How could looks be so deceiving?

He looked down at her and smiled, showing off large white teeth. "I will try to make this as quick as possible. But, you see, I have a torture that needs to be implemented while you are alive. I'm afraid it won't work on a decomposing body. If you feel that you must scream from the pain, please do so. I will understand. I chose you to be the captive held on the stretching rack. Over the next several hours to days, I will stretch your body. Unlike in the actual torture, I will allow you to rest your backside on the table. I have set up a rack to stretch your arms and legs. I will start slowly. As time goes by, I will speed up the process."

Sienna looked at him in horror. This man was crazy.

***

The woman's long arms and legs would be perfect to display on the rack. He tortured her just enough to make the body look gruesome, but not so much that visitors wouldn't believe that she was still alive and being tortured. In the stretched pose, her magnificent breasts added a sexual tone to the display.

He'd discovered a large wooden wheel at the back of the property that would be perfect for what he had in mind. It was rather large, though, and would take some effort to move in here. He would hate to break it down in order to move it. He may have to have the medieval torture room downstairs so that he could fit the wheel in a room. The old sitting room off the back may be the perfect place for it.

Chapter 8

Gregory answered Thomas Billiot's call on the second ring. Thomas started talking immediately, "I know you are busy, but Grace is planning a dinner party over here Friday night. I was calling to see if you can come."

He replied, "I wouldn't miss one of Grace's dinner parties for anything."

"I think she is playing matchmaker again. I wouldn't bring a date if I were you."

Gregory groaned, "Didn't she learn from her last failed attempt?"

Thomas let out a deep laugh. "My friend, the one thing you should know about my wife by now is that she never gives up. She is determined to find you a wife."

Gregory shook his head, "Not me, I am a confirmed bachelor."

"I said the same thing."

Gregory stated, "Ah, but you married the last sane woman. Do you know what is on the menu? I can at least bring the wine."

"She has a full seven course menu planned. She mentioned lobster thermidor, beef Wellington, risotto, roasted asparagus, and chocolate mousse."

"My mouth is watering already. I don't know how you stay so fit."

With a broad smile on his face Thomas replied, "I find ways to work it off."

"I can only imagine, mon ami. I will see y'all on Friday night. Tell Grace to go easy on me, please."

"I'll try, but don't hold your breath." Gregory knew his friend's wife meant well, but he didn't see a woman being interested in him and his perverse business. The women were interested briefly, but then that interest died fast when they realized how obsessed he was with the haunted houses. Especially when he showed them how warped and twisted his mind was. What if they were to find out just how dark he really was?

Friday arrived quicker than he wanted. He despised breaking away from the haunted house. It was taking longer than he'd anticipated. Moreover, he didn't wish to spend time entertaining one of Grace's friends that she had decided would be perfect for him.

Hopefully, she would soon run out of friends to fix him up with. As he left his house, his stomach let out a loud rumble. He'd watched what he'd eaten today, so he could gorge himself on Grace's amazing cooking.

He was about to ring the doorbell when Grace burst out the door and hugged him tight. "You have been a stranger lately. You know with all that money you pull in from the haunted house you could hire someone to help you so that you aren't always so busy. How will you meet someone if you are always working?"

Gregory looked down at her and laughed, "Now Grace, you know I am too much of a control freak to let someone else build my props for me. I would never trust that they were doing it the way I want."

Grace shook her head at him, "You should at least hire an assistant to help you. You look so tired, and you still have several months before you open the doors once again."

"I have considered hiring an assistant, but this is such a cut throat business that I just don't know if I can trust anyone. What if another haunted house chain has sent the person over to spy on me? I can't take that chance?"

Grace held up her hands in surrender, "I can tell I will lose this argument. At least come in and make yourself comfortable. You can have one night to relax and enjoy yourself, can't you?"

Gregory bent down and kissed her on the cheek, "I always make time for you and your cooking."

She shoved him on his shoulder gently, "Flattery will get you everywhere with me."

She grabbed his hand and pulled him along, " Come on; I have someone I want you to meet."

Gregory moaned in protest, "Now Grace, you know I don't like blind dates."

"What blind date? This is a friend of mine who I invited to join us for supper."

He asked, "Uh huh and how many other friends did you invite to supper tonight?"

"I wanted to keep this party small and informal, so it's just the four of us. Now stop dawdling. Thomas is pouring us a drink as we speak. Caitlyn is a very sweet girl. I'm sure the two of you will get along splendidly."

As he walked past the kitchen, he remarked, "Smells great. What time are we eating?"

Thomas heard Gregory as he neared the den, "Get your ass in here. I need someone to drink this scotch with me. These women want wine of all things."

As soon as Gregory walked into the den Thomas slapped him on the shoulder and handed him a scotch. "Good to see you man. You've been a stranger around here lately."

"So your wife tells me. I've been busy setting up the new haunted house."

Thomas asked, "So tell me, when do we get to see this new haunted house?"

Grace brought Gregory over to Caitlyn, "Enough business talk. Gregory, I would like you to meet my very best friend, Caitlyn Reed."

Gregory took her hand in his, "Very nice to meet you Ms. Reed."

Caitlyn stood up, "No, it is my pleasure to meet you. I have to admit that I am a huge fan of yours."

Gregory was surprised when she stood up. She was almost looking him in the eyes. She had the bluest eyes. He could get lost looking into those depths, "So, you know who I am then?"

"Oh my, yes. I don't miss an opening night. I am a huge horror junkie. Where other women may like the romance books, I want the horror. The gorier the better. I must admit that I have tried to decorate my house for Halloween, but nothing I have done has come close to what you do. You have to tell me some of your secrets."

Thomas laughed, "Gregory wouldn't tell the pope himself his secrets. He keeps his prop making process locked away from the world in that mind of his. The man is paranoid that his competitors will send spies over. He had yet to let anyone know the location of his next haunted house."

Caitlyn let out a gasp, "You are opening another haunted house? Oh, you have to tell us where it is."

Gregory loved her enthusiasm. He almost let it slip, "You will just have to wait. I'm not ready to divulge its location. Maybe when it is almost done."

Caitlyn was intrigued, "Are you keeping the other one open?"

Gregory stated, "I am. It is pretty much on autopilot now. I hired a manager to work it this year. He will start the day before it opens." Gregory hoped that the new manager wouldn't become too nosy and look at the props in depth.

Thomas chuckled, "You don't know how hard it was to get him to turn the reins over to another person. He kept thinking he could open one later than the other, that way he could be present for both opening nights. I had to convince him he would lose money that way."

Gregory looked over at his friend, "Money isn't everything. These are my babies. I have poured my blood, sweat and tears into the haunted houses. I hate to see them in the hands of another individual."

"Mon ami, as your empire grows, you will have to learn how to delegate. You will run yourself ragged."

Grace walked back in to announce that dinner was served. "Why don't we finish this conversation in the dining room?"

As the evening continued, Gregory had to admit that the dinner conversation and the company were great, but it was getting late and he needed to excuse himself. "Thomas, ladies, while this evening has been great I need to get back. I still have several projects to catch up on. I'm behind on some of my deadlines."

Caitlyn stood up, "I'm sorry that you have to go. I hope that we meet again." She retrieved her purse from a nearby chair and reached into it and found one of her business cards. "Here is my number. If you ever find yourself in the area and would like some company give me a call."

Gregory took the card from her but didn't let go of her hand. Instead, he pulled it up to his lips and gave it a kiss. "I would be delighted to. I do find my way to this area at least once a month. Maybe we can get together. I'll give you a call next time I am around." Gregory turned to Thomas and Grace, "Thank you for an enjoyable evening."

Grace walked over and gave Gregory a hug, "Don't be a stranger."

Gregory kissed her cheek, "I won't."

On the way back to Point Creole, Gregory decided to search for another subject for his Halloween props.

He pulled over to one of his favorite corners. Darkness enveloped this area. As usual the security light was not working. The humid night air hung heavy with the promise of rain. The sliver of a moon barely illuminated the sky.

***

The noise of the surrounding bars filled the night air. Terri Adams had been working this corner for two years now. The other girls knew to stay clear, and if a newbie tried to move in on her territory, she showed them who was boss.

Terri had often been told she resembled a man more than a woman. She sometimes believed she should have been born a man. She was over six feet tall and well built. Growing up, the other children picked on her relentlessly. However, living out here on the streets, she could be whoever she wanted to be and not be judged.

The skin on the back of her neck prickled with warning. A noise from behind startled her. The figure appeared from the shadows. He simply stared at her, not saying anything. His eyes glittered in the dim light that was cast from the

moon. A shiver of apprehension snaked down her back.
She felt a jolt of electricity flow through her body.

Several hours later, Terri snapped her eyes open wide. Bile
made its way up her throat, burning as it traveled upwards.
Blood coursed through her veins as fear built inside of her.
She soon realized she was restrained to a table. Her head
felt heavy, her hands clumsy. Her body refused to
cooperate.

Her eyes darted around the room, trying to ascertain where
she was. She looked to see if anyone was lurking about.
She kept waiting for someone to leap out and begin their
assault on her body.

***

This prop would be perfect for his meat locker. He wheeled
his stainless steel cart closer to have easier access to his
tools. There was no need to torture this one. He picked up
the CO2 syringe and injected it into her neck.

He needed to gut her like a fish. Before he could remove
the bones, the blood needed to be drained. Using the
embalming machine, he drained the body of blood.
However, for this prop he did not need to add the
embalming fluid afterward. Next, he carefully removed the
bones from her body. After he was done, he sprawled the
eviscerated remains on two tables. He began applying the
beeswax over the body, making sure not to miss a spot.

It was a painstaking process. If the end results were what
he'd envisioned, then it would be worth the extra time he
had put into this prop.

With the prop complete, he needed to bring her into the room he had prepared. He inserted the prop into the meat hooks attached to the ceiling. Near opening day, he would add the intestines, blood and other organs to the room. Her skeleton would be reassembled and used in the graveyard.

After he had secured her on the meat hooks, he stepped back to admire his work. It came out better than he had imagined. She appeared to have been gutted, just like a wild animal, and was hanging to be cured.

Chapter 9

He watched as she exited the club and stepped into the darkness of the night. The cloudless sky was ablaze with twinkling stars. She was perfect for what he had planned. She had a face that would have inspired even the most cynical of artists. Her body was ethereal, but contained a hint of sensuality. He could close his eyes and imagine what her skeletal structure looked like. Hers would rival any of those he already had.

He had her room prepared. The main door to the bathroom from the hall had been replaced with Plexiglas so he could watch her as she died. He wondered how long it would take her to succumb to her death. She would be perfect for the scene he wanted to portray, unfortunately for her, she must starve to death to achieve the end result.

***

The area was cloaked in shades of black. The noise of the club faded as she headed down the street. All she wanted was to kick off her heels and relax. Candi was a no show tonight, and she had to pick up the slack.

Olivia Carlson had been working at Cherry's for almost a year. If it were not for the fact that she needed the extra money to help feed her coke habit, she would quit.

A noise from behind startled her. The skin on the back of her neck prickled with fear. She slammed a hand to her heart as terror took over her senses. A figure appeared from the shadows. He stared at her, not saying anything.

She felt a jolt of electricity pass through her body as she dropped to the ground.

She wasn't sure what happened. At first, she hadn't noticed, but as the fog lifted from her mind, she realized she was locked inside a bathroom. Her head felt heavy, and her hands clumsy. Her body refused to cooperate. Why was she here?

She saw the man approach the glass that separated them. "You have been chosen for a spectacular prop," he informed her. His voice chilled her to the very core of her being. She cringed in fear. "I wish there was a pleasant way for me to achieve this, but, unfortunately, I can't think of any other way than to starve you to death. Just think of the incredible fame this prop will bring you."

There was a coldness in his eyes that terrified her. This was not how she wanted to die. Goosebumps covered her body. She shivered in terror.

Chapter 10

Gregory pulled into a truck stop to grab a quick bite to eat. A young girl captured his attention. She appeared to be moving from one truck to another looking for a ride. She would be perfect for one of his props. She had fabulous bone structure.

He carefully approached her, so as not to frighten her away. "Miss, you do know it isn't safe to bum a ride from some of these truck drivers don't you?"

She looked up at him with the most pitiful eyes. He could tell she had been crying, "I don't care. I need to get away from this town. My stepdad is a monster, and my mom won't listen to me."

"I tell you what, why don't you let me buy you something to eat, and then I will give you a ride out of here."

"For real?" She looked at him in skepticism, "I don't have to do anything with you, do I?"

He chuckled, "All I require is that you eat whatever you order."

"Thanks a lot, mister. You don't have to drive me too far. As long as you get me the hell out of here."

"I can do that." If she knew what he had planned for her, she would be very wary of him.

***

The feeling of being cold, extremely cold, was what woke her. She began to shiver. Something wasn't right. It wasn't supposed to be cold yet. Her mouth felt dry and she was so thirsty.

As she opened her eyes, she fought back dizziness and nausea. Darkness surrounded her. She started to panic. She was deathly afraid of the dark. She reminded herself to stay calm; panicking would not help.

A foul odor penetrated her senses. It smelled rotten, as if something was decaying in here.

 She observed her surroundings with grim determination. Fear gripped her body. She had to force herself to breath slowly. A complete feeling of hopelessness took over her. She had to get her emotions under control. Hysteria would do her no good.

She heard footsteps echo through the room. A light came on, and a man approached her. Whatever he had in mind, she knew it wasn't good. She didn't want to die. If only she could wake up from this nightmare. The psychotic demon looked so familiar. Then she realized it was the man from the restaurant. Why was he doing this to her?

***

Ferris let the knife blade tickle her skin. She tried to squirm away from the tip. Ever so gently, he slid the blade across the skin of her belly. She screamed in agonizing pain when he moved the knife up her body and slowly drew a line of blood. The blade teased her skin, barely penetrating it.

For this prop, he needed to have the body branded. He picked up the branding iron he had heating. She had felt the heat from the metal before it touched her flesh. Once it made contact, the pain was instantaneous and astounded her. The air smelled of burning flesh and blood.

Mascara streaked down her cheeks, mixing with her tears. "Please let me go. I won't tell anyone."

The sorrowful expression was what he wanted. Acting quickly he injected her with the CO2.

Before he could work on the prop, he needed to drain the body of blood. He set up the embalming pump. As the pump removed the blood, it would refill the body with embalming fluid.

He needed to reshape her mouth, so it appeared as though she died with a scream on her lips. He also needed to let the body decompose some. It would take longer with the embalming fluid, but it gave him time to stretch the body. He would check on the progress every few days until he achieved the final result.

Chapter 11

Olivia Carlson bolted upright. Where was she? What woke her? Then the realization hit her; she was trapped in this place.

She tried to ignore the sounds haunting her. They were like fingernails on a blackboard; deep, violent and nerve racking. Whatever was making the noise was coming from the stairs; it always seemed to come from the stairs. The sounds never let up. It was a constant noise.

It had been a while since she last saw him. At least she thought it had been a while. She had no way of telling how much time had passed. She couldn't remember how long she had gone without food. The only thing keeping her alive was the water she got from the tap. The hunger pains were constant now. Most days all she had the strength to do was sleep. She couldn't survive much longer without food. She could see her bones now. When she looked in the bathroom mirror, she didn't even recognize herself.

She heard footsteps approaching and backed away from the opening. There was a place to hide in this room, away from his prying eyes. With each step, her heart raced faster. Evil seemed to surround the man who'd abducted her. When she looked into his eyes, they were soulless.

At night, an eerie light seemed to fill the old house. She wondered what he was doing, but she was too afraid to ask. She might not want to know the answer.

She had always been an independent person, not wanting to depend on another individual for even the basics in life. But now she would give anything to have someone care for her. To have someone she could depend on for all the necessities in life.

Why was he doing this to her? She never thought someone could be this demented. What made a man like him be this way?

Her whole body ached from being confined in this space for so long. She was too weak to exercise.

Chapter 12

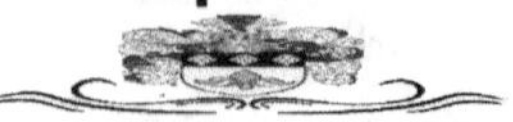

Ferris entered the strip club on a mission. As he sat down, he saw his next subject dancing on center stage. In his mind, he went over which prop her luscious little body could be. His skin tingled in anticipation of what he wanted to do to that body of hers, and it didn't involve sex. He didn't need to rape any of his models; they were of no interest to him. He had a long line of women who were willing to warm his bed.

He pulled out a fifty-dollar bill and tucked it into her G-string. That should get her attention. As she moved closer to him, he caught a whiff of her perfume, a heavy floral scent. She had a pouty expression on her face when she looked at him. He would love to make her frown a permanent one.

"Come on, sugar, let's move this little party to a private room in the back."

This would give him the perfect opportunity to slip a drug into her drink. "Order us some champagne." He pointed to his pocket, "I have a little something else you can have as well." He could tell from her red nose that she had a drug habit. He knew from experience she wouldn't turn down free booze or drugs. The combination of the sedative mixed with the drugs would make her easy to slip out of here.

After he had her back at the plantation, his eyes roamed over the restrained woman. She was still unconscious from the drugs. Once he removed the awful wig, a luxurious mane of auburn hair was revealed. Her voluptuous breasts, small waist and tight rear did nothing to excite him, but they would make the perfect mannequin.

He preferred to kill some of his subjects while sedated, while others he preferred to torture first so that he achieved the correct expression on their faces. She would be his sleeping beauty, so while she slept he injected her with the CO2 cartridge.

He craved his time in the plantation making his dream become a reality. It was his special time. It was the only place where he could be himself. There was no one to judge him or his sick and twisted fantasies.

This was where he found true fulfillment. In here, there was nothing but him, his thoughts, and his fantasies. It was his personal paradise. Being here rejuvenated him, renewed his focus, and gave him strength.

Tonight he planned to spend hours on his projects. Dividing his time between each scene and working on perfecting them. Some of the scenes were proving to be more difficult than others.

Chapter 13

Ferris let the cigarette smoke slowly leave his mouth as he waited and watched for his next subject. He was propped up against a corner that headed into an alley. His car was parked deeper in the alley. It didn't matter to him the sex of the next subject. It would be whoever approached him first.

The night sky was a shimmering mass of twinkling stars. The full moon cast a soft glow across the street. He blended into the shadows just enough to give him mystique and waited for someone to approach him.

The latest newspaper article on his haunted houses, while good for publicity, had put his face into the limelight. He couldn't have someone recognize him.

He noticed a young man fast approaching him. He perked up; this could be the one. He took another long hard drag on his cigarette and waited.

***

Matthew Chapman needed a hit. He had been walking these streets for over two hours searching for someone who would help a desperate, but broke individual score drugs. At this point, he would have sex with anyone for a score.

He saw a man standing in the shadows, watching as those around him went about their business. Maybe this guy was a dealer and would give him a small hit. It couldn't hurt to ask. "Hey mister, I don't mean to bother you, but I need a hit. I can't pay you, but I can offer my services to you. I need it bad man."

"Come over to my car. I got exactly what you need, free of charge."

At first Matthew thought he was dreaming. No one gave away free drugs; there had to be a catch. "What's the catch?"

"Send some business my way. Tell your friends where you got a good deal on some drugs."

Smiling, he told the man, "I can do that. I really appreciate it, sir."

***

When they reached his car, he had the syringe ready. In one swift movement, he injected the young man. As he fell, Ferris caught him and shoved him into the trunk. He did a quick survey of the area to make sure no one noticed. Satisfied that he was safe, he closed the trunk and drove away.

Once back at the plantation Ferris placed him on the table. He studied the man to ascertain how he wanted the prop to look. Then it came to him. He would have blood dripping from his eye sockets, and all that stared back at you were hollowed out eyes. He would also have the prop clawing at his face, with bone glistening beneath the shredded skin.

Chapter 14

Kelli Thomas never saw a man emerging from the shadows. Her head was yanked back as he wrapped his strong arms around her neck and lifted her small frame in the air. She felt his hand covering her mouth and nose. Something in his hand smelled sweet.

Her heart hammered with fear. Her mind was reeling, what was happening? This couldn't possibly be happening to her now. Not when she had finally saved up enough money to leave this hellhole and could make a life for herself. She struggled to free herself.

Tears burned her eyes, but she refused to let them flow. She tried not to breathe in whatever drug was doused on the rag. Trepidation took over, replacing every sensation in her body. She kicked and twisted, trying frantically to free herself from this maniac's grip. He was too strong, and she was becoming dazed from the drug. She was losing her battle to stay conscious; the drug was taking effect. Soon oblivion wrapped her in its warm embrace.

Kelli awoke slowly as the effects from the ether began to wear off. Her eyelids were heavy and her mouth dry. Her arms and feet were secured to a table of some kind. She had been disrobed and was laying spread eagle. She tried to pull free from the restraints, but they were too tight.

Now that her vision had cleared, she noticed that she was in a workshop of some sort. She strained to see if she could make out any sounds. She heard nothing but a deafening silence. She started to panic; her heart beat faster. She yanked on the restraints one more time, but they refused to budge. All she'd accomplished was to cut into her wrists and ankles. When she moved, pain shot through her.

 Kelli struggled to remember what had happened to her.

A door opened and she heard footsteps fast approaching. The man who entered the room was a good-looking man, handsome actually. She never considered that evil could be so handsome. Evil should be menacing, a repugnant monster. She now knew that evil could take on the look of many faces. It isn't always apparent when looking at someone to know what is hidden inside their soul, their true self.

"Please don't hurt me." Kelli saw the knife in his hand and panicked. Her heart pounded inside her chest. "What are you going to do to me?"

Ferris placed his finger to her mouth, "You will be one of my greatest accomplishments yet. You see, you are in the workshop of my haunted house. I make specialized props for the rooms. I have chosen you for my next scene. Unfortunately, you do have to die for your body to become a masterpiece. I will try to make this as painless as possible, but some of the cuts have to be done while you are alive. I don't get the same effect when blood is no longer pumping through your body."

Kelli had had some appalling things happen to her in the past, but nothing like this. This made being raped by her drunken stepdad seem like child's play. Nausea washed over her as she tried to move.

Maybe Kelli's mom had been right and she was a bad girl. After all, weren't bad girls the ones killers flocked to in the movies?

She felt the knife cut into her skin; the blood oozing out of her. It would be so easy to close her eyes and succumb to death. Let the darkness wash over her, vanquish the years of pain. A primal instinct bubbled up inside of her, the fight to survive conquered the desire to surrender and die. She wanted to live. She was starting a new life for herself.

She let out a gut wrenching scream and struggled to break free from the restraints. The pain became all consuming. She used the pain to keep her focused. Somehow, she had to escape.

"Perfect. This is just what I am looking for." He grabbed the CO2 cartridge and injected her as she was about to scream. This may be one of his best pieces yet.

Chapter 15

It was time for him to search for another subject. The crowded strip club would be the perfect hunting ground. There had to be over twenty girls on the center stage dancing and even more girls on the floor serving drinks and mingling. Everyone appeared to be in the party mood tonight.

Ferris knew women looked at him and drooled. He was the whole package, the athletic body and good looks. None of his subjects were scared of him in the beginning. It was only when they woke and saw his true self that they became afraid.

As he walked around, he finally found the perfect woman. She had a tantalizing, curvaceous body. A smile stretched across his face. Yes, this one would make a perfectly wicked prop.

***

Bambi had been on her feet for hours dancing. Work was rough tonight, and she wanted to go home and crash. She thought this would be an easy way to help pay for med school, but after tonight she was reconsidering that idea. Was the money worth it?

Bambi looked at the man who walked up to the stage and decided the night was looking up. She could get lost in his eyes. His body was sheer perfection, nice and tight. "Haven't seen you around here before. New in town?"

"Just passing through and looking for a good time."

"Well Hun, you came to the right place." She continued to dance in front of him, being as seductive as she could.

She whispered in his ear, "I get off in a few minutes. Care to hang around?"

"I'd love to," he replied.

***

Smiling, he thought to himself how easily he'd lured her in. As he watched her dance on stage, he thought about ways to display her body.

He had wanted to experiment with one of his props, skinning a body to show what it looked like underneath the flesh. She would be the perfect specimen, and he was very interested in getting her back to his workroom.

When they got into his car, he forced the rag over her mouth. He gave her a substantial dose. He didn't need her alive. It would be better if she were dead by the time he arrived home so he could begin work immediately.

Ferris always thought of his prop making as a hobby. Now, after thinking about this in depth, he knew it was a calling. It had taken root and become an addiction. Several other haunted house companies had asked him if he could make them props as well. They loved how realistic his look was, so much better than the ones they bought. If they only knew. He could never sell his. Upon close inspection, he would be found out.

Before he could work on skinning the body, he needed to drain ninety percent of the blood. He wanted to leave enough so the body still had a pinkish tone to the flesh, without worrying about too much blood ruining the prop.

He wheeled the cart holding his surgical instruments closer to her. Selecting a scalpel, he began to skin his victim, being mindful of his actions, not wanting to mar the body any more than he had to. He would use the skin for the walls of the morgue.

Looking down at the prop after he was finished, he was quite surprised at the results. He had the larger pieces of skin stretched and drying. He was proud of what he had accomplished. He had two props for the price of one.

Now he needed to coat the body in beeswax so it didn't lose the appearance he had worked so hard to achieve.

Chapter 16

Alex Jameson wasn't sure how long he had been working these streets, but it had become pure torture. When he closed his eyes, all he saw was blue water and white sand. For April, it remained quite cold. He had considered hitchhiking somewhere south where he wouldn't freeze his balls off while waiting for a john.

It'd been a while since he had a hit and instead of looking for a paying customer, he scanned the streets for a drug dealer. They were always close by, waiting to jump on a sale.

The powerful addiction to meth was pulling him in more and more. It was getting harder to think of anything else. He took greater risks to pay for his habit. Lately, it had been near daybreak before he went back to his pitiful excuse for a home. He was staying in an old abandoned building. The only thing nice about his new habitat was that no other street dwellers had found it yet. The city had forgotten about the abandoned building. The electricity was off, but there was still running water.

From the corner of his eye, he noticed a man leaning on the wall leading into an alley. Alex walked his way. The man's demeanor had him believing he had drugs he could buy. From a distance, Alex studied him closely to make sure he wasn't an undercover cop. Some were getting good at their disguises and you didn't know they were cops until you felt the handcuffs on your wrists and he was dragging you to the precinct. Once he made sure that the stranger was not a cop, he went over and asked, "Do you have something to get me through the rest of the day?"

***

Ferris looked at the man with curiosity. He would make a perfect manic depressive in the asylum. He may be able to keep this young man in one of his "rooms". He could hold this one prisoner and let him be a live exhibit to charge at the crowd as they passed. "In my car, it's not too far from here."

***

As Alex woke up, something felt off about his surroundings. He didn't remember walking home last night. Whatever he took gave him one hell of a hangover. He felt as if he had been run over by a truck, not once but several times.

Shadowy demons danced across the room as the moonlight shone through the window. Ghostly feet creaked across the old floor downstairs.

A hint of alarm reached him when he realized he was not back at the building where he usually slept. He thought he heard someone talking to him, but the voice sounded muffled. "Ah, good, you are awake. I have chosen you to be one of my performers. Please make yourself comfortable, this room will be your new domicile for the next few months. I need to make sure you go insane in order to pull the scene off just the way I want it. The best way to look at your situation is that while you are here you will get your meals paid for along with a clean room and a bed."

Alex charged at the glass separating him from the man hoping to break free. It was a futile attempt. The glass refused to budge.

"You can try to escape, but I promise you there is no way. This is your new home, like it or not."

With sickening clarity, he knew he was doomed. This man would not let him escape. He would finally pay for the sins of his past.

Alex had often dreamed of being stranded on a secluded island. Now that he had the opportunity to be kept away from people, he felt the loneliness set it. He had always been told men don't cry. He ignored that comment and let the tears flow.

***

Alex could no longer remember how long he had been held captive. The days had blurred into one. He despised this feeling of complete powerlessness. He had to depend on this man for food and water. Living on the streets, he should be used to going to the bathroom wherever he needed to, but the smell in this tiny room was beyond repulsive. He feared that at any moment he would go insane.

Chapter 17

He saw her walking out of the local coffee shop and stopped. He had never seen a more perfect specimen for his haunted house. She brought a new meaning to malnourishment. He had a feeling if he could get her to smile he would find that her teeth had rotted out from drug abuse. It was still early in the morning; most of the town was just waking. She was more than likely getting ready to crawl into a hole somewhere and sleep. He followed her closely. If his suspicions were correct, this coffee was her breakfast, probably the only thing she could afford, and she was homeless. Over the years, he had learned to spot the people that would not be missed and could join his collection of props.

He followed her into the alley and acted quickly. He knocked her unconscious with ether and tucked her behind a dumpster. He rushed back to retrieve his car and loaded her in the trunk.

***

Kim slowly woke. Where was she? Everything was one big blur; nothing came into focus. Her arms and legs appeared to be strapped down to a table. The air was icy and damp against her skin. What was happening?

She desperately tried to wiggle free from the straps. She heard footsteps and possibly someone talking. Her heart sank; if her captor was here then there was no way to escape.

***

Ferris thought he'd given her enough ether for her to be out for a while. He had given her enough to kill a horse. Although he had learned that serious drug addicts had a different reaction to the sedatives he used. Nevertheless, he would inject her with the CO2 cartridge so he could prepare her for the scene.

***

She screamed when she saw her captor walk towards her with the needle. Fear built up inside of her. She was not getting out of here alive.

Chapter 18

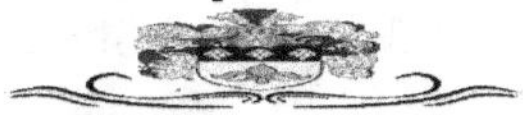

Darkness shrouded the back of the bar. The businesses were far enough apart that he didn't have to worry about being seen. He knew from experience that most of the dancers would come out back for a smoke between shows.

He saw two dancers walk outside and wondered if he could capture both of them. It would be risky, but if he could pull it off, the outcome would be perfect. The haunted house was coming along nicely, and if he could double his subjects tonight, it would ensure he met his deadlines.

He had the ether rag ready to go and reached into his pocket for the stun gun. The stun gun should knock out the smaller one, but his timing had to be perfect.

He opened the car trunk so that he could load them into his car.

Walking up to the women, he asked, "I'm sorry, but do either of you have a spare cigarette? I seem to be out." He held up a box and shook it to prove that it was empty.

One of the girls held out a pack of cigarettes, "Here sugar."

Acting quickly, he moved in. He grabbed the one closest to him and aimed the stun gun at the other.

***

Star wasn't sure where they were. She didn't see Amber. As her vision came into focus, a man appeared in front of her. She noticed something gleaming in his hand. It looked like a knife. She looked at his face again and noticed his eyes; they were dark and soulless. She could feel the evil emitting from him.

"I'm glad you are awake. I have such plans for you and your friend. I am thinking conjoined twins."

Terror tore through her body. She heard a deep moaning. "Amber is that you?" Star knew they were going to die. The sudden realization filled every molecule of her body. Tears rolled down her face as the knife slipped into her flesh. The pain was red hot. Blood flowed down her body. It had a warm sticky feeling to it. A blackness washed over; she knew she was losing consciousness.

***

Looking down at the prop after he had finished, he was surprised at how well it had come out. It had been rather easy to conjoin the two women. He had joined them at their backs. They would be displayed on a slow rotating device. One woman would be exquisite, and then the other would be horrendously disfigured. The one called Amber had been the luckier of the two; she died with no pain.

Chapter 19

The haunted house was coming along, but he wished he could work faster. He looked out the window and watched as the shadows danced across the massive lawn. He sometimes wondered if he was no better than a serial killer. He felt no shame or remorse for what he had done to achieve his masterpieces. He was sure the Halloween props he had created this year would astound everyone. He had let his imagination run wild, conjuring up horrific visions and creatures.

The pneumatics were working properly, as was the computer system that would ensure everything went off as timed. He had no doubt this would be a tremendous success.

He looked down at his wristwatch and was surprised to find that it was four o'clock in the morning. He had worked through the night again. His body was heavy with exhaustion. He should rest so that he could finish a few more of his props later.

However, he had two bodies to break down for parts before he could stop for the day. He laid the tarp down and pulled out his tool kit. Over the years he had learned how to break down a body just as fast as a butcher preparing a pig or cow.

The saw cut through the bone, chewing and grinding. He had previously drained the bodies of blood. It was still messy work, but not near as messy as a body full of blood.

Chapter 20

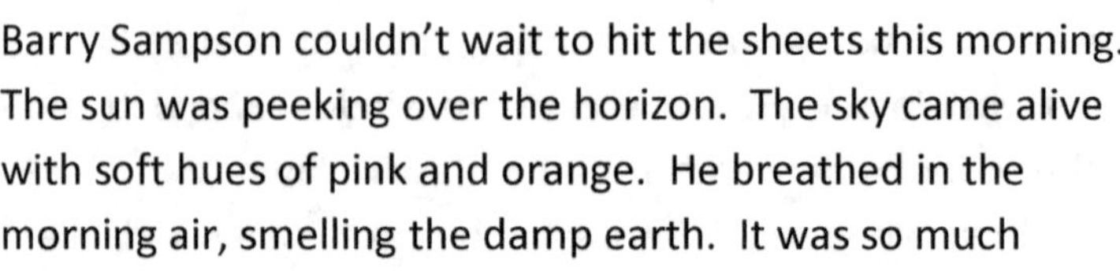

Barry Sampson couldn't wait to hit the sheets this morning. The sun was peeking over the horizon. The sky came alive with soft hues of pink and orange. He breathed in the morning air, smelling the damp earth. It was so much better than that stuffy bar.

A shadow fell across Barry as he rounded the corner. Before he could react, a jolt of electricity shot through him.

***

Sunlight filtered through the trees. It was supposed to be a gorgeous day. Rain or shine, he knew it would be a glorious day for him. The bouncer from the bar was huge and would make the perfect subject. He didn't know if someone would miss him or not, but by the time he was missed, Ferris would be several states away.

The hulk of a man was heavier than he appeared. He was pure brawn and would take more wax than the others. His mind was reeling as he thought about how he wanted to arrange this scenario.

On the drive home, he spotted a deer in the road. The poor animal must have been killed on impact. Seeing the dead animal gave him an idea that was true inspiration.

He would have a taxidermy room where various animals were used for experimentation. He needed to set out several traps to capture the local wildlife.

His mind was reeling with possibilities. Then it struck him.
This big hulk of a man could be the slave master. He would
give him a truly powerful role. With his dark skin, he could
apply white paint on his body and face that would appeare
perfect in the black light.

He would also have a woman bound to the ceiling by her
arms from hooks. He would have to find the perfect woman
for the part. She would have to have several visible whip
lashes applied to her body so that he could create the effect
he desired.

If he closed his eyes, he could imagine the man raising his
whip and giving the girl lashes across her bare breasts.
Maybe one should be partially mutilated? Yes, that may
work.

This was his favorite part, creating the scenes. As time went
by, he usually added little details.

He walked upstairs to check on his guests that were
currently staying with him. He smiled when he heard the
stairs groan as he walked. He was very pleased with his
choice to create a haunted house here. It was almost as if
this house talked to him and it had lots to say. Creaks,
moans and thumps regularly sounded throughout the
house. It helped create the perfect atmosphere.

As he walked down the hall, he realized he could still put a
few more live subjects in several of the other rooms. He did
need as much live entertainment as possible. The crowd
got a charge from people trying to escape, begging them for
help. They played their roles to such perfection.

After completing the prop, which took an ungodly amount of time due to the bouncer's sheer size, he was ready to work on the taxidermy room.

He broke the deer down to prepare it. He planned to replace the deer's legs with human arms. He had removed four arms from the freezer to make this freak of nature. He also decided to combine a woman's upper body with a man's lower half. The top half of the male body would be used for a zombie breaking out of one of the subterranean graves. The woman's lower body would be exposed to the visitors in the slave master's room, with several lash marks on it.

He was also preparing a body that sat on the floor with his legs tucked up under it; his head would be turned backwards. One hand would be on his head and he would have the spinal cord revealed. Along with hands on each shoulder and three other hands showing on each side, giving the creature nine hands showing along the back of his body.

If he didn't rein in these ideas of his, he wouldn't be ready for opening day.

Chapter 21

Caitlyn heard her doorbell ring and sighed. She wanted to sit here and sulk for her birthday. She looked through the peephole and was surprised to see Gregory Ferris. He had a large bouquet of white roses with Asiatic lilies and pink tea roses.

She opened the door, "This is a nice surprise."

He kissed her on the cheek and handed her the flowers. "A little birdie told me it was your birthday and that you were a little depressed."

Caitlyn opened the door wider for him, "She is such a blabbermouth. Please tell me that she didn't tell you how old I am."

"She may have mentioned why you wanted to forget about this birthday."

"Jeez, I guess nothing is sacred. Come on in. I'm not ready to turn a year older. I thought I would have more accomplished at this point in my life."

"Well, you don't look like anyone close to thirty. You are simply ravishing."

Taking the flowers from him, "Well, thank you. These are beautiful".

Gregory asked her, "Let me take you out to supper, please?"

He pulled her along with him, "I don't know. I'm not even dressed to go out."

"You look just fine. Come on, you still need to eat, don't you?"

"I guess."

He escorted her outside and opened the car door for her. Caitlyn was impressed with the Bentley Continental GT. It was her favorite color as well, red. "I didn't take you for the Bentley type."

He grinned, "I am a car fanatic. When this car came out, I had to have one. It has a V8 and handles the road superbly."

Caitlyn laughed as she ran her hands along the soft leather interior. "So you are into haunted houses and expensive cars. The haunted house business must pay pretty well."

"It didn't start out as a money making business. I had to pour a lot of blood, sweat, and tears into it. I guess that is why I have a hard time turning over the business to someone. Plus, I am an extreme micromanager."

"So where do you plan on taking me for supper?"

"I also heard you like Italian food, so I called and made reservations at Nemo's."

Caitlyn stated, "That is one of my favorite restaurants. I guess Grace told you that and all kinds of other information about me."

Gregory admitted, "I may have asked her a few questions when she asked if I could help cheer you up. Although, Nemo's is one of my favorite restaurants. I love their lasagna and the pizza."

The ride to Nemo's was quiet. Neither knew what to say.

Caitlyn laid her head back against the headrest and let the luxury of the car relax her. She took in the beautiful night. The Mississippi River was on her side, and she watched as the moonlight danced across the languid waves. She became lost in the slow, steady waves as they caressed the bank.

She was pleasantly surprised that Gregory Ferris showed up at her door. She felt the car slow down and realized they were at their destination. "I'm sorry I was lost in my own little world."

Gregory looked over at her, "It was nice just having you beside me. You look so cute sitting there."

Once seated, Gregory ordered a bottle of Chianti and antipasto.

Caitlyn tasted the wine, never having been a fan of Chianti, but she had to admit that it was very good. "So I have to be nosy, what made you get into the haunted house business?"

"Growing up I always loved Halloween and begged my parents to let me decorate the house spooky to scare the neighborhood kids. I was an outcast and scaring the crap out of them that one night was my revenge for them taunting me during the year."

Caitlyn laughed, "For some reason I can see you doing that."

"One year there was a bully who bothered everyone. He wouldn't let up, so I planned something special just for him. I had to enlist a friend to help though. We had everything set up and scared him so bad that he peed in his pants in front of everyone. It was priceless. My friend happened to have his camera and took a picture. The guy never bothered anyone again. In fact, the geeks of the school started picking on the bully."

Caitlyn couldn't help but laugh, "And let me guess, Thomas was your partner in crime?"

"He was. How did you know it was Thomas?"

"Ever since I met the man he has always seemed to be a shutterbug. When I asked him about it, he told me that he never knew when he may get a chance to take the perfect picture and wanted to be prepared. Now it is starting to make sense."

"Thomas and I have been friends since we were five. He has always had a camera in his hands. When we went off to college, I thought for sure he would take journalism or photography, but he didn't. He said that it was just a hobby."

Caitlyn stated, "A very good hobby though. Have you seen some of his latest pictures?"

Gregory nodded his head, "He took the pictures for my advertising shots. I wouldn't trust anyone else."

They talked and laughed for hours as if they were old friends. She told Gregory about her family, hopes and dreams. How she hoped to one day find a love just like her parents, someone that would be with her through thick and thin.

Gregory told her his dreams of opening haunted houses in several more locations, if he could learn how to relinquish some of the control. How he was a nomad, never staying in any one place for an extended period of time. How he liked to travel and see different areas of the United States. How he suspected this was because his parents were such recluses.

The night passed by quickly, and before they knew it, the waiter was telling them that they would be closing soon. Caitlyn was surprised, "I didn't realize we had been talking so long."

Gregory escorted her back to his car, "It has been a very pleasant evening. One I don't want to see come to an end."

"Same here, I can't think of the last time I had such a pleasant date."

Gregory asked, "Would you like to get together again?"

"I'd like that very much. When will you be back in town?"

Gregory kissed her hand, "For you, I can make it here more often than normal."

"Are you able to tear yourself away from your newest haunted house?"

Looking directly into her eyes, "Most definitely. I can't remember the last time I had such a pleasant evening talking to another individual. And to think, I was ready to strangle Grace for attempting another setup."

Caitlyn giggled, "I take it her previous attempts have been total disasters?"

Caitlyn noticed the twinkle in his eyes, "Let's just say a root canal would have been a more pleasurable experience."

"That bad, huh? I must say I was petrified when she told me she had someone she wanted me to meet, but then when Thomas told me who it was I couldn't say no. Thomas knows I am a huge fan of yours, but he never mentioned that they knew you."

"Thomas and Grace know that I like my privacy. I still haven't gotten used to the fame associated with the popularity of the haunted houses. When the magazine article came out, I couldn't walk down the street without someone recognizing me. I don't think I left my house for a month afterwards. Thomas told me to embrace the fame."

When they arrived at her house, Gregory went around and opened the car door for her. He took her hand in his and escorted her to the front door. He placed a finger under her chin and tilted her face up, bending down and kissing her gently, "Happy birthday, Caitlyn."

She was speechless. The kiss, although gentle, shook her to the core. She looked into his eyes and could see the desire building. She waited for him to kiss her again. Instead, he took the keys from her and unlocked the door, "Thanks for the company tonight. I'm glad I decided to surprise you for your birthday. We will have to do this again.

Caitlyn watched as he drove away, wondering if she would hear from him again. She hoped so, because she was still reeling from the goodnight kiss.

***

Gregory looked at the clock. It was still relatively early for the hookers working downtown. Since he was falling behind on his schedule, he needed to get his hands on some more props. He had a particular scene he was anxious to complete. It was coming together nicely, but it was lacking something. He didn't have time to search up north, so he would look locally. He was likely to find someone here that would fill his need. He had to be extra careful in how he arranged this prop. When searching for subjects this close to home, there was a chance that someone might recognize them, even if it was a slim chance.

The night air had Ferris feeling alive, or could it have been the perfect dinner he'd had with Caitlyn. Should he pursue a relationship with her?

The moon was a bright orb hanging in the black sky, stars twinkled in the background. He considered turning the car around, and going back to Cailtyn's, but an urgency to finish the scene pushed him forward. From a distance, he saw a man limping, heading toward a dumpster. Ferris was intrigued. This may be just the subject he needed.

***

Stephen Breaux had been a high school football legend. He had several colleges begging for him to play for their team, offering him full paid scholarships. His old man had hopes of him going pro, but Stephen didn't see football as his career. He wanted to serve his country and joined the Air Force. If he could go back in time, he would have gone to college and played football. Maybe then he wouldn't be suffering from post-traumatic stress disorder and afraid of his own shadow. He may not have seen the same amount of action as those that served in the Army, but being in the medical field, he had to treat their injuries. Their battalion was on the way to the hospital one morning when they were ambushed. The explosion cost him a good friend and one of his legs.

When Stephen returned home, he couldn't step back into his life before the Air Force. All he had before joining was football and he couldn't play football with a leg missing, no matter how hard he tried.

If he had listened to his parents and taken the love and support they had offered, maybe he wouldn't have turned to drugs and alcohol to numb the pain and forget the past. After several attempts at trying to help him see reason, his parents gave up on him. Now, here he was twenty-seven years old and homeless, digging through dumpsters hoping to find booze or food. Either one was fine with him. Booze was always better though.

The stillness of the night was eerily peaceful, a peacefulness that would be soon taken over by pure evil. Stephen couldn't remember the last time downtown had been this quiet; it was as if everyone besides him had something important to do.

The hairs on the back of Stephen's neck rose, he swore someone was watching him. His nerves were strung tight tonight, but he envisioned he was back in combat. He could feel a predator's eyes upon him, watching his every move. *Stop it! You have been doing well without reliving the past. You are back on U.S. soil and safe.*

He stopped and listened. He could barely make out the sound, but it sounded as if footsteps were coming up from behind. Before he could react, a man appeared. He felt a jolt of electricity tear through his body.

***

The man was lighter than Ferris first assumed. He tucked him behind the dumpster while he retrieved his car.

While loading him, Ferris discovered the reason for the limp. The man was missing one leg. This man may indeed be just what he needed to complete his scene.

***

When he woke, Stephen waited as his eyes came into focus. He had to adjust to the darkness. He observed his surroundings with grim realization. His hands and feet were bound tight and it felt as if he were in a moving vehicle. More than likely he was being held in the trunk of a car. Fear surged through his body. He had to force himself to breath slowly. A complete feeling of hopelessness took over. He had to get his emotions under control. Bringing on a panic attack would do him no good.

When the car came to a stop, all he could do was wait. A
man opened the trunk, "You shouldn't be awake just yet.
I'm sorry, but you are perfect for the scene I have started in
my haunted house."

****

Ferris had hoped to kill the man in the workroom, but with
him awake and alert he had no choice. He looked through
his bag on the back seat and found a spare CO2 cartridge.
He went back to the trunk of the car. By now, the man was
kicking his legs in a frenzy.

****

Stephen knew that whatever this man had in mind, it wasn't
good. When he first lost his leg, all he thought about was
death. Now that there was a chance he may die, he was not
ready. This was such a nightmare, one he couldn't wake up
from. As the needle punctured his skin, the pain became
excruciating. Death was quick though.

Chapter 22

A row of Leyland Cypress trees hid the bar from the shopping center. Ferris assumed the shopping center owner didn't want his shoppers worrying about the patrons of the bar. The trees also offered the perfect cover while he watched and waited for the opportune moment to strike. The inky blackness of the night allowed him to lurk in the shadows unnoticed.

The haunted house was almost complete, and the girl who walked outside to smoke would be perfect. He had a feeling that this year he would make a nice profit. This haunted house may be better than the one in Springport.

He needed a crazy woman sitting on a rocking chair, rocking and mumbling to the crowd. From the looks of her, she would do nicely.

***

The first thing Claire Berkshire noticed when she woke was the putrid smell. Where was it coming from? It reminded her of the dumpster outside the club, but worse. She kept telling herself to open her eyes, but her eyelids were too heavy. It was still dark wherever she was. Blinking, she tried desperately to clear her vision.

Her heart was pounding in her chest. She seemed to be locked in a small room with a bucket in the far corner. A rocking chair was in the middle of the room, and there was an old, ratty, flannel blanket on the seat of the rocker. Apprehension rose inside of her.

She tried banging on the glass, but it was solid. The smell became more repugnant the closer she got to the glass. It smelled as if something was dead. *Come on girl, wake up. This is just a nightmare. You are stoned out of your mind, that's all.* She tried to remember what had happened to her. The last thing she remembered was stepping outside of the club to smoke.

She heard footsteps approaching, "I'm glad to see you are awake. I didn't think you would ever wake up. I have a special part for you in my haunted house and you don't want to disappoint me, I promise you that. When the time comes, I need you to sit in this rocker and act like a demented woman. To help you get into the part, I wanted to give you time to adjust to the setting."

Chapter 23

Claire Berkshire hated being caged like an animal. This guy had a screw loose. She swore she heard others moving around and screams kept her awake at night. She was starting to lose her mind.

With each passing day, she became more sluggish. Her mind and body were fatigued beyond the point of return. All she wanted was to close her eyes and sleep. The foul and fetid odor that had surrounded her no longer bothered her. She wished she could fall asleep and never wake up from this nightmare. She had lost count of how many days she had been here. How long did he plan to keep her caged?

He hadn't tortured her and he kept her fed, but that was it. He brought her just enough food for her to survive on, so death was not something he had planned for the time being.

The wind blowing through the rafters wreaked havoc on her nerves, and the moonlight cast foreboding shadows that danced across the room. From her room she could see the other rooms, and it terrified her. She wondered if the mannequins were real or very good displays.

She heard a distinct rustling near the doorway and this time it wasn't the wind. Squinting through the glass that barricaded her in, she peered into the dark hall to make out what the noise was. Was that footsteps? Was the maniac back? The hairs on the back of her neck stood up. He was back. He appeared to be carrying a horrendous torture device.

The incessant hammering and sawing he was doing grated on her nerves. Evil seemed to surround her captor, seeping from his very pores. If only she could cover her ears and drown out the noise. Sweat clung to her skin, drawing the bugs to her. They bit into her tender flesh. She tried to swipe them away, or at least scratch the places where they had bitten. The constant itching was driving her insane.

At times, the eerie silence was worse than the terrifying screams. She wasn't sure which was worse. She just wished she were any place but here.

Chapter 24

Caitlyn walked in the door and kicked off her shoes. Today had been one of the most trying days she had had in a long time. Normally she enjoyed working at Buds and Bouquets, but today nothing went right. The new florist Mr. Pierron hired messed up on the Fermin wedding arrangements. She sent the arrangements for Duke Harvey's funeral to the wedding and the wedding arrangements to the funeral home. It had taken over an hour to get that mess sorted out, and there were plenty of upset customers as well. The day didn't get better after that. The girl didn't have any people skills, and several customers flat out refused to deal with her and insisted on waiting for Caitlyn, which infuriated the girl.

Caitlyn considered opening her own business, but she could never afford it in New Orleans. She barely made ends meet as it was, and the added stress of opening her own business could bankrupt her. For now, she was stuck working for Mr. Pierron, which wasn't so bad. He was a nice man who treated his employees well. She had worked there for almost five years now, and she had never had any problems with him. He had always treated her fairly. Her only concern was the newest florist, and hopefully she would start to fit in.

She checked her home phone to see if there were any messages. She had been hoping that Gregory Ferris would call, but so far he hadn't. She thought that the date had gone well, but maybe she'd read the signals wrong.

Caitlyn decided to call Grace to see if she had heard from Gregory. Besides, she hadn't called to thank her for sending him over for her birthday. Grace picked up on the first ring, "I was just thinking of calling you. Did Gregory surprise you for your birthday?"

Caitlyn informed her, "That is why I am calling. I haven't had a chance to call and thank you for telling him about my birthday. He surprised me with flowers and dinner at Nemo's."

"So, how did it go?"

Caitlyn felt like a teenager asking her friend if someone had a crush on her, "I thought it went great. We talked until they closed the restaurant. He was a perfect gentleman and I thought for sure it had gone well. I'm starting to wonder though, because I haven't heard from him since he left that night."

Grace let out a sigh, "That sounds like Gregory. I love the man to death, but when he starts working I don't think his mind thinks of anything else. You will have to be patient with him."

After hanging up with Grace, she went into the kitchen to prepare a quick supper. Looking through the fridge, she grimaced. She needed to go grocery shopping. She would have to settle on the last of her mom's gumbo. Once it was warm, she took the bowl and headed to the living room. She may as well catch up on some of her recorded shows before the DVR was full. She started a show and curled up on the couch.

No matter how hard she tried to concentrate on the show, her mind drifted back to her dinner with Gregory the other night. As she was finishing supper, the phone rang, "Hello."

"Caitlyn, it's Gregory Ferris. I didn't catch you at a bad time did I?"

She responded quickly, "Oh no. I'm sitting here trying to unwind from a hectic day at work."

"Would you like to get together for supper, maybe on Friday night?"

Hoping she didn't answer too quickly, she blurted out, "That would be great. I wasn't sure if you were taking too much time off right now."

They ended up talking for several more minutes before finalizing plans for Friday night. He made her feel like a teenager with a crush. She wondered why someone like him was still single. He seemed to have it all; good looks, money and personality. She hoped he wasn't hiding a dark skeleton in his closet. She could see herself falling in love with this man.

Chapter 25

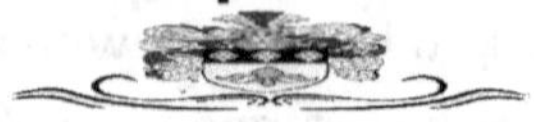

Dear God, please let me die. I'm ready to die, to end this suffering. Alex Jameson imagined himself on a beach, a tropical island far away from here. He wanted to escape reality. If only he could return to that dream.

When his captor brought him his lunch, he pleaded with him, "Please let me out of here. I can't take it anymore."

"You're an integral part of this haunted house. The show won't be anything without you. I can't let you go."

Despair took over his senses. He was never leaving this place alive.

"Please, you have to let us go!" Alex begged as the maniac walked away. God only knew where they were being held. Fear twisted inside him like a knife.

Alex knew the chances of any of them escaping were slim. There was no reasoning with this psycho. He was truly depraved. Alex had never suspected anyone of being able to do anything this vile.

"Please I'll do anything. Please just let me go," he hollered out, trying to keep his voice from shaking in fear.

The monster kept putting food in each of the rooms. Alex was certain that he was drugging the food. He was always groggy, especially after eating, and he spent most of his time sleeping.

Nevertheless, he was grateful for the mind numbing fog because it helped him tune out the screams and various noises that seemed to plague this old house. The brief time he was awake, he feared that it would be his turn to die. Even through the fog, at times he could hear others crying and begging to be let out. He wondered how many others were held captive. No one answered when he asked for names; maybe they were too afraid to talk.

The days ran together. Day in and day out he lived in a dreamlike state. It was somewhere between wakefulness and slumber. He had become so desperate for human conversation that he had begun talking to himself.

He prayed that God would send someone to free them from this house of horrors. As each day passed, he feared his prayers would go unanswered. Maybe God had yet to forgive him for the sins he had committed. He tried not to lose faith. God was omnipresent; he would save them! Didn't the Bible say God forgave all who asked? Tears ran down his face as he prayed, begged God for forgiveness. Even as the words left his mouth in a silent whisper, he knew they were doomed.

Chapter 26

Ferris lurked in the shadows, hidden by the trees alongside the brothel. He couldn't risk being seen there. He doubted anyone would worry when a girl went missing. No one would call the police, they wanted to keep knowledge of this place a secret. There were no exterior lights around the house; the exterior was bathed in darkness. The anticipation of creating another scene sent tingles down his body.

***

Yvette Hampton hated her job, but if it weren't for Miss Chloe she would be out on the streets peddling her ass for any Tom, Dick, or Harry. At least here she had a roof over her head and three square meals a day. Moreover, there was security inside if a man tried to get too fresh.

If only she hadn't gotten so upset with her parents and stormed out of the house when she was sixteen. Back then, she thought she knew everything, but was she ever wrong. Pride kept her from calling her parents to ask if she could please come back. It had been three years since she ran away, and every night she wondered if they missed her. She wished she could go back home.

Yvette stepped outside to take a smoke break before her next customer. She never saw the man lurking in the shadows. Before she could scream, he had his brawny arms around her and the ether soaked rag pressed against her mouth and nose.

***

As Ferris placed his newest subject into the trunk of the car, he was already imagining her in the snake's den. He needed to get the look of fright frozen onto her face at the perfect moment. He had the rest of the scene already set. It would look like a ghostly area of the bayou. He found several cypress trunks around the plantation, as well as an old bateau. As he did in the voodoo room, several oak branches dangled from the room with Spanish moss dripping from the branches. The floor was painted pitch black with bits of moss thrown on it for good measure. There were several ferns placed around the room, making sure that the pots holding them were hidden.

He would have it look as if she were chained to a tree branch from overhead while the snakes slithered up and down her. This room would be a perfect scare, especially for those who were deathly afraid of snakes.

Once he was back home, he made sure she was restrained. When she woke, he would begin to frighten her to death. He knew which expression he needed when he killed her.

***

Yvette woke up to the feeling of being tickled. As she became fully awake, she realized it wasn't a tickling sensation as much as something crawling up and down her skin. As her vision came into focus better, she was paralyzed with fear. This had to be a nightmare. How did she end up being covered in spiders? And was that a snake? She tried to brush them off her. When she went to move her arms, she realized her arms and legs were restrained. Terror gripped her body as she watched the spiders crawl over her body. She was too afraid to scream. She didn't want the spiders to crawl into her mouth. She tried to clamp her legs shut to keep the nasty little things from exploring her body.

***

Ferris enjoyed watching the show, but if he wanted to get anything accomplished today, he needed to hurry. Stepping closer to her, "I see you met my newest addition to the haunted house. I'm sorry it has to be this way for you, but you see, I need you for a particular project and these new friends of yours will be joining you."

He wondered how long it would take for her to scare herself to death or die from a spider or snake bite. Ferris wasn't sure which spiders were considered poisonous. He wasn't even certain that he had a poisonous spider in there. They could all be deadly. From the way she was thrashing around on the table, he would say they were more than likely sinking their fangs into her flesh at this moment. The expression on her face was priceless. He picked up the CO_2 cartridge and injected her neck at just the right time.

Chapter 27

Ferris knew people hated spiders. He had found different ways to attract them to the house to set the mood. By the time the haunted house was open, people would be running for their dear lives, desperately wanting to get away from here. If everything went right, word of mouth would have a line waiting at the door. People, especially the younger generation, loved to get scared.

It had taken longer than he expected to get everything ready, but now that it was coming together, he was anxious to see the end result. He was proud of his props. They would wow the crowd with their gore factor. This place would be filled with pure visceral horror; fear that would have a physical effect on the crowd.

A massive, unbreakable aquarium had been set up in one room. From a small area in the top right corner, he'd made an access point to insert the snakes he captured. The snakes were easy to obtain. They were plentiful around the old plantation and bayou. It didn't take him long to fill up the aquarium. He had a very nice collection with several varieties. The snakes were easily annoyed and struck at the glass. This should scare people as they passed.

Before sealing the room, he made sure his centerpiece was ready. She came out better than he could have ever imagined. By the time she died, she had numerous fang marks covering her body. He had been worried that the wax would hide most of the marks, but instead it intensified the effects. It was spectacularly chilling.

Ferris looked around at the scenes playing out. He immensely enjoyed the perverse pleasure he received from creating each prop. He was perfecting his skills. If he needed them to look more dead rather than alive, he waited until they decomposed before applying the wax. The decomp also helped make the feel and smell of the house more realistic.

Before going out in public, he would stop by his rental house in town to shower the smell off. He also purchased a cheap car that he used besides his Bentley. He didn't want to get the smell of decomp in the Bentley. He also had an old four-wheel drive truck that he took on the old gravel roads around the plantation. Soon he would hire someone to blacktop the entrance. He preferred to keep the feel of the gravel driveway, but it might be a deterrent to some visitors. It was beginning to look like a haunted house.

Chapter 28

It was the simple things in life that Claire Berkshire missed. She would never take anything in her life for granted after this ordeal, that was if she survived. What she wouldn't give for a watch to tell the time. At least she had a window so she could catch a glimpse of the outside world. But she wanted to feel the sun on her face.

It would be heaven to see a newspaper or turn on the TV. She wondered what the date was. How long had she been in this hellhole? At first she had counted each sunrise, but lately they'd blended into one.

She wondered what she looked like now. She felt as if she was melting away. She tried washing herself the best she could at the sink, but there was no soap. She missed even the bare makeup essentials, the feel of gloss on her lips.

It would be nice to be pampered at a beauty salon. Her hair was a mess. It hung loose; limp and lifeless.

She felt the drugs taking effect. Her mind was going blank, and she was exhausted. She welcomed the darkness. It was her brief escape from this hell. She was having trouble focusing on the real world. She found herself slipping further into her dream world. Her sanity slowly slipped away.

Chapter 29

As Harry Stanford walked home, he wondered where his life had gone wrong. He had been popular in high school, all-star quarterback, dated the cheer captain, and even married her. Now he was alone and working dead end jobs - whenever he could keep them. In retrospect, he should have paid more attention to his wife and kids. Then maybe his wife wouldn't have left him for his best friend. Now his kids wouldn't have anything to do with him, and his wife was finally happy and sharing her bed with another man. A man who treated her better than he ever did.

After his world had come to an end, he'd turned to alcohol. Now he was a constant drunk, living in a crappy motel room and broke. He'd lost his last job and hadn't been able to find another job. No one wanted to hire a dead beat. He had become a joke around town; everyone probably talked about him behind his back. As he contemplated his life, he wallowed in self-pity. If he had done things differently, maybe he would have a happier life.

Fog and a pitch-black night made visibility almost impossible. A light rain was falling and even the moon and stars were hidden. He was alone as usual. Perhaps the world would be better off if he ended his life. His kids were entering their teenage years, and since the divorce, they had nothing to do with him. A chill swept through his body. He swore he'd heard footsteps coming up behind him. He stopped to listen, but there was only silence. Looking around, he saw nothing but emptiness. Maybe the booze was playing tricks with his mind. Suddenly an electrical shock traveled through his body.

Harry woke slowly. He opened his eyes and tried to focus on his surroundings. His head felt as if it would split wide open. He was lying on his stomach with his arms and legs tied together behind him. The restraints were too tight. He couldn't pull himself free. He finally calmed his nerves and tried to figure out where he was. It felt as if he was in a moving vehicle. He was almost certain of it. He attempted to buck himself free, but the way he was hogtied made it impossible.

Harry noticed the car had stopped moving. He heard footsteps approaching. From his current position, he had no means of protecting himself. He was having a hard time breathing. Why had someone kidnapped him? He had no money, no one would pay to keep him alive.

Once again, he tried to break free of the restraints. If he could free himself, when the trunk opened he might escape. There had to be a way out of this mess. He needed to calm down and think.

When the trunk opened, Harry saw the large needle in his abductor's hand. The color drained from his face. There was no escaping this. He was going to die.

***

Ferris had felt the movements in the trunk and heard his subject grunting. His captive was awake. This wouldn't do at all. He found a quiet place to pull over. He reached into his bag and grabbed the CO2 cartridge. He had hoped to keep this man as a member of the cast, but he would have to wait for another cast member. Besides, he could never have too many props.

Ferris despised killing this far from home, but he didn't have a choice. He would have to drive through the night, and hope he arrived home before the smell of death permeated his trunk. Now he regretted driving the Bentley. He would have to stop by a supermarket on the way home. If nothing else, he would get bags of ice to slow down the process. Dry ice would be even better. It should help keep the body cold longer.

On his way home, he thought about the dead man in the trunk. He could create a gory autopsy scene with this body. He wondered if he could preserve the heart and other organs. He had some formaldehyde at the house. He could display the organs in jars on a table in the back. He'd found a pair of tree pruners when cleaning up outside that should cut through the rib cage. Yes, this scene may play out quite well. He would need to think of a few ways to make it more gruesome. He had been draining the bodies of their blood and saving it in an old refrigerator. It worked sporadically, but it kept the blood cool. He had been freezing several of the organs after removing them, so this may work out even better than he had originally planned. He would need to experiment, but he now knew that an autopsy room would be added to the haunted house.

Chapter 30

The putrid odor of death roused her from her unconsciousness. The darkness started to lift. The stench was so potent now that it caused her to gag. She tried to take small shallow breaths, trying not to breathe in the foul odor. She hoped it wasn't her that smelled that bad. She couldn't remember the last time she'd had a shower. She had lost track of time; she could no longer remember how many days she had been here. If only she could escape.

Tears built up in her eyes, threatening to spill. The darkness that surrounded her diminished. She wished she could go back to sleep. She tried to think of anything other than the overwhelming stench.

She tried to ascertain what had woken her. As her vision improved, she realized he was at it again. He was hammering and using a saw. She had no idea what this place was, but she was confident that evil lived here.

She saw something slither across the doorway. There were snakes in this place! They were everywhere.

She heard him yell, "Son of a bitch!"

***

Ferris couldn't believe it. The last bunch of snakes he'd caught from the bayou somehow managed to escape from the burlap sack. Now he had to round them up and place them in the room. He couldn't have them slithering around. He believed he'd captured only rat snakes this morning, but

he couldn't be certain. He didn't want to come face to face
with a pissed off poisonous snake. Of all the rotten luck!
Just as he was getting the autopsy room the way he wanted
it, he had to stop and take care of something else. At times,
he seriously wished he could bring in an assistant, but there
was no way. He couldn't trust anyone to share his secrets
with. This was the price he must pay to have the most
incredible props.

Chapter 31

Caitlyn was ready for tonight. She didn't think Friday would ever get here. She was falling hard for Gregory. She'd picked up some protection and put clean sheets on the bed this morning, just in case.

She even took off from work early so she could take an extra-long time getting ready. She had called Grace last night to let her know that they would be having an actual date tonight, and to thank her once again for setting them up. The man was hot. Who wouldn't want to date him? They seemed to be perfect for each other.

Butterflies fluttered around in her stomach as she waited for him. You would think this was their first date as nervous as she was. She had opened the door before he had a chance to knock. He bent down and kissed her lightly on the lips. It left her wanting more.

Caitlyn couldn't stop talking on the way to the restaurant. She chatted nonstop and hoped that she wasn't talking too much. From the smile on his face though, she still had his attention. He looked enamored not bored.

When they arrived at Josephine's, she noticed the line. "This place seems to be popular tonight. I'm not sure we will ever get a table." She had never seen the line this long. It wrapped around the corner of the building.

He took her elbow and escorted her to the front door. People stared at them as they walked inside. After Gregory gave the hostess his name, the maître d appeared, "Right this way Mr. Ferris, it's good to see you again."

Caitlyn looked at him in surprise, "You must have some real pull around here. I didn't think they took reservations."

He looked down at her and smiled, "They don't, but I know the owner. We have a special table for tonight."

The maître d escorted them to a private room near the kitchen that was bathed in candlelight and flowers, "Oh my," Caitlyn gasped, "This is beautiful."

Gregory informed her, "I didn't want to share you with the other diners. I want a nice, cozy dinner so we can sit and talk."

"I wasn't expecting such VIP treatment. A girl can get spoiled being around you." She glanced around the room in awe. She felt like a princess.

He smiled over at her, "I'm so glad you agreed to go out with me again. I was afraid after ignoring you that you wouldn't answer my call."

Caitlyn wondered if Grace had called and asked him if he was going to call her back. She would be mortified. She had to call Grace and find out if she did, in fact, call him.

Caitlyn couldn't take her eyes off Gregory. He looked dashing in his suit and tie, but she suspected that he could make a burlap sack look good.

She sometimes wondered if the way she felt wasn't love, but awe, from the attention he lavished on her. She didn't remember anyone treating her this special.

Gregory looked across the table at her and smiled. That simple gesture caused Caitlyn's heart to leap. No, she was almost certain that she was falling in love with him.

Caitlyn was annoyed that Gregory had taken it upon himself to arrange the menu ahead of time, but after tasting the filet mignon, she forgave him. It melted in her mouth. "Now I understand why the lines are always so long to get into this place. The food is excellent. It is well worth the wait."

Gregory agreed, "The food is excellent, but no one can compare to Grace's cooking."

Caitlyn agreed. "If I were Thomas I would weigh four hundred pounds. I do good not to burn a grilled cheese sandwich. What about you? Are you a master chef?"

Gregory laughed at that remark, "Thomas and I starved ourselves to death until he started dating Grace. Neither one of us could cook. I burned food in the blink of an eye."

She chuckled, "You can't be that bad, can you?"

"I'm pretty bad. Toaster ovens don't even like me. It was easier for me to warm up soup in the microwave than to burn down the house trying to cook."

"My biggest problem is cooking for one. It seems easier cooking for more than one person, or at least not as depressing."

"I have done it for so long now that it has become second nature to me. I scare off women when they find out what I do."

Caitlyn laughed at that comment, "I can't imagine why they would be afraid of you. I sometimes wonder what goes on in that mind of yours. Some of those creatures you come up with almost look life-like. You must have one hell of an imagination."

"I have loved doing things like this for as long as I can remember. I dream of different creatures for the haunted house at night. I have so many ideas floating around my head, just not enough time to complete them all."

"I can't wait to see your new haunted house. I bet it will be even scarier than the original."

He looked at her with a smile on his face, "That's what I am aiming for. If I could keep my mind on one project at a time, I could get more completed. As opening night gets closer, I start panicking that things won't be finished in time."

"It will be great. I can see a line several miles long of people anxiously waiting to get in."

Caitlyn didn't realize the time until she saw the lights turn off in the dining room. Gregory looked at her, "It's after one o'clock. I didn't realize how long we have been talking. I guess I need to take you home so that you can get some rest."

Caitlyn hated to see the night end. She wondered if she should ask him in for a nightcap. As he'd previously done, he escorted her to her front door and kissed her lightly on the lips, "Goodnight Caitlyn. Sleep tight."

"Goodnight Gregory."

Caitlyn's heart sank as she watched him drive off. She had chickened out and never asked him in for a nightcap. Now she regretted it. She wouldn't be getting much sleep tonight as she tossed and turned thinking of Gregory.

Grace called Caitlyn the next morning, "How did the date go?"

Caitlyn asked, "You didn't call and ask if he was going to call me again, did you?"

"Honestly, I didn't. But, I did talk to him this morning. He completely adores you."

Caitlyn let out a sigh of relief and laughed at herself. "I think I'm falling for him."

Grace felt giddy over the fact that she may have a successful couple match, "I think he has it bad for you too."

Caitlyn thought he would have made a move last night, but instead he kissed her goodnight at the door. At first the fact that he was such a gentleman turned her on, now it was becoming annoying. She wondered if he found her sexy.

Chapter 32

Gregory looked at the clock and realized that he still had time to search for another subject. While he wanted to stay and kiss Caitlyn longer, he didn't want to scare her away. It had been a long time since a woman was this captivated by him. He wanted to take it slow.

He was afraid that if he stayed with her for too long that he would let something slip about his hobby. Caitlyn may be comfortable with his inept interest in haunted houses, but she might have a problem with his selection of figures for his props. He didn't think many people would be comfortable with how he made his props.

He made his way back downtown and parked in a dark alley. After locking the car, he went in search of another perfect subject.

***

Kim Stevens was walking back to her hotel room. It was a pleasant night for a walk. As she neared the street that the hotel was on, she swore she heard someone behind her. A shiver snaked down her spine. Turning around, she didn't see anyone. She continued walking, but picked up her pace.

She heard the footsteps again, and her heart jumped into her throat. She looked around, but didn't see anyone. Was her mind playing tricks on her?

Strong arms grabbed her from behind. She tried to scream, but a strong hand clamped down on her mouth and nose.

He was holding something against her nose, forcing her to breathe in whatever he had saturated the rag with. She tried to fight him off, but her attempts were futile. She lost consciousness, slipping into darkness.

***

He loaded her up into the car and headed back to the plantation. Once there, he brought her up to the room where she would be staged. Normally he preferred to prepare his props in his workroom, but this time, for him to make it look realistic he needed the blood splatter to be just right. He would do his magic here, and once she was ready to be waxed he would move her to his workroom to finish the process.

He had a large hook on the wall that would hold her in place. Once she was secured, he walked to the entrance of the room to ensure everything was as it should be. He stared at her and envisioned how this room would look. From where he stood, it looked as if it may be missing a wow factor, but perhaps after he finished with the body it would be perfect.

***

Kim tried to figure out where she was. She remembered walking home, but wherever she was, it wasn't her room. Her legs and arms ached and when she looked up, she found her arms shackled to a massive hook on the ceiling. She screamed when she saw a large man standing not too far from her. Just the sight of him had her frozen in fear. She looked at him closer and realized he wasn't moving. Swallowing down her fear, she wondered what was going to happen to her. She attempted to free her arms from the hook above her, but it was useless. She couldn't free herself.

Her toes began to ache so she tried resting them, but this increased the strain on her wrists. Her captor entered the room and stared at her nude body. "Please let me go," she begged him.

He ignored her and continued walking around her. He informed her, "I'm sorry that it has to be this way, but it is the only way I can make this as realistic as possible."

The way he said this caused something inside of her to snap, "What the fuck do you think you are doing?'

He shrugged at her outburst, "You will play a significant role in my haunted house."

A chill swept over her body. She looked at the mannequins in the room one more time. Could they have been alive at one time?

She watched as he walked over to the large male mannequin and removed the whip from his hand. Genuine fear snaked up her body. "Please don't," she begged.

She heard the whip crack through the air and then felt it sting her flesh. Tears fell from her eyes, smearing makeup down her face.

He walked in front of her, "I will try to be gentle with the lashes, but I need to mar your beautiful skin." She couldn't believe that was gentle. The pain was excruciating. She couldn't imagine anything worse.

As he continued, Kim no longer wondered how long she had been suffering through the lashes of the whip. The pain was intense and unrelenting. She no longer felt her hands as the blood flowing to them had stopped. Cramps had developed in the back of both legs and all she could do was sag forward.

Her back felt as if it was on fire. This was not a normal position for a body, and with each lash of the whip, she was amazed that the pain could be worse. Blood ran down her back and splattered on the walls and the ceiling. Her mind could not comprehend that this was happening to her.

Chapter 33

Gregory Ferris drove into town. Now that it was late July, he needed to advertise the haunted house. He would start here and then expand his advertising.

He had a printer in New Orleans print over a thousand flyers for him to hand out at various places. He would start here and expand more each week. Maybe as he looked for new subjects.

He walked in Creole's Diner and sat at the bar. Margie, one of the waitresses, walked over to him, "Morning. Can I get you your usual?"

That was one thing he loved about small towns; the waitresses tended to remember what the regular customers ordered, "But of course. Nothing beats the grilled pork chops and eggs here."

"Coming right up, sugar. I'll bring you a cup of coffee."

"Thanks, Margie."

When she came back with his coffee, he asked, "Hey Margie, do you think there would be a problem with me leaving a flyer or two about the haunted house?"

She laughed, "So that is what you are doing at the old plantation. Rumors have been flying around town since you bought the place. Several people figured you were fixing it up to live in."

"No, I am in the haunted house business. I was looking to expand, and this area seemed like an excellent location. There isn't a haunted house attraction for miles around."

"Mon Dieu, Halloween is a big thing around here. The teenage kids travel all the way to New Orleans to get the crap frightened out of them. I think you may be on to something. Mais oui, leave a few for people to share."

"Thanks, Margie. I hope I don't offend anyone here, though."

"Don't worry about them old fogies. These kids need something like this. It is better than them driving to N'Awlins. Plus, it may bring some business to the town."

As soon as Gregory put out the flyers, it seemed to catch everyone's attention. He had several people stopping and asking him about it while he ate his breakfast. It may be a bigger success that he first suspected. He needed to call the printer in New Orleans and have them print more flyers. He would have flyers sent to the neighboring towns to be included in the Sunday newspapers.

***

Mike Newsom stopped at the diner on his way to football practice to grab a soda. He saw the flyer and grabbed one to bring to the school. This was what this town needed, something to do for Halloween. Besides, he had been trying to find a way for Cyndi Blanchard to run into his arms, and this may do the trick. He hoped it wasn't a lame haunted house that a two year old could walk through. He wanted one that made you run screaming into the night.

Chapter 34

Caitlyn was trying to decide what she wanted to do for the night when the doorbell rang. Wondering who it was, she looked through the peephole and her heart swelled when she saw Gregory, "This is a nice surprise. I figured you were busy at work."

"I thought I would take a little time off and show you a night on the town."

Caitlyn smiled up at him, "That sounds fantastic. I was just trying to decide what to do. Do we have time for me to change?"

"Take as much time as you need."

Caitlyn reached up and kissed him on the lips before dashing to her room to get ready. As she entered her room, she told him, "Make yourself at home. I won't be long."

Gregory walked around the living room, trying to get a better feel for the woman who had him intrigued. He couldn't get his mind off her, when he should be thinking about the haunted house. Since he wanted to spend more time with her, he would search for props here in New Orleans, which could be dangerous. He was being extra careful, but he hoped that someone didn't come into the haunted house and recognize a face on one of the props. So far, he believed that everyone he had captured from around here had been disfigured so badly that even their mothers wouldn't recognize them.

He heard Caitlyn exiting her bedroom and met her in the hall, "You clean up quite nicely. You look stunning tonight."

Caitlyn blushed at the compliment. She grabbed her purse and keys on the way to the door. As they walked outside, she saw the limousine, "What's this?" she asked.

"Your chariot awaits cher. I thought we would have a night on the town and be spoiled while doing it. We can go bar hopping or whatever you like, and not worry about fighting for a parking spot."

"This sounds like pure heaven to me. I've never indulged in something like this before. You are spoiling me way too much."

The chauffeur held the door open for them. Once they were situated, Gregory opened a bottle of champagne for them to enjoy. "I want to enjoy your company tonight and this allows me to spend all of my time with you."

Caitlyn was flattered by the sentiment. She may have found the perfect man for her. She couldn't find the first flaw in him.

The evening went by quicker than she wanted. She didn't want the night to end. She had enjoyed sitting this close to him. She could feel the desire for him building inside of her. She wondered what it would feel like to be held tight in his arms. What it would be like for him to make love to her. Would he be as attentive as he was right now?

Gregory asked her, "I have to come to New Orleans on Wednesday. I know it is a work night for you, but would you be available for supper?"

"Sure. Why don't you come to my house and I'll have something for us to eat."

Gregory picked up her hand and kissed it, "I don't want to put you out. I can take you out to eat."

"It's no problem. Don't worry, I won't give you food poisoning or anything, I promise."

Caitlyn felt the limo stop and knew that they were back at her house. She hated for the night to end, but knowing that she would see Gregory again in a few days sent a thrill through her.

Gregory escorted her to the front door and kissed her harder than the previous times, "Until Wednesday night then."

"I'll be counting the minutes."

"I'm not sure what time I will be over here, but it is likely to be sometime after six o'clock."

Caitlyn informed him, "I will be here. I get off work at five o'clock."

He kissed her one more time before he left. Caitlyn watched as the limo pulled away and wished it were already Wednesday.

***

Gregory shook his head as the limo driver drove back to the hotel where he'd picked him up from. He had arranged for the limo to prevent him from spending the night at Caitlyn's place, and somehow he found himself arranging a date for

Wednesday, even though he had no plans to come this way in the middle of the week. He must have it bad.

As he walked to his car, he saw the perfect subject.

Chapter 35

The moment he turned the corner onto Front Street he knew he was a dead man. A chill ran down his spine warning him of the upcoming doom.

He had known for years that someone would end his life while he was still young. He lived a dangerous life, and that was a chance he had to take.

A shadow stepped directly into his path. He started to shout, but never had time to utter a sound. A jolt of electricity shot right through his body. He felt himself crumple to the sidewalk.

As he fell, he could still hear the music playing from the festivities on the bayou. A musician played a jazz piece that filled the air.

***

Ferris looked at this man as he loaded him into his trunk. He would do nicely for what he had planned. His upper body was built like a tank; he could envision him as the devil in the basement with the tortured souls.

By the time Ferris arrived home, the man in the trunk was awake. Not wanting to bother sedating the man another time he grabbed a CO2 cartridge and injected him. This prop would take a lot of time, time he was already short on. At least he'd previously started carving the horns from bone. With the man's head being shaved, it would save him some precious time that he had so little of.

Ferris also needed to rub the red pigment dye on his body and add it to the beeswax. He wanted Satan to be a bright red with black eyes. He'd found a pair of glass eyes while online one night and ordered them just in case he did create the devil.

Exhilaration hummed through Ferris's body as he prepared this prop. It was such a thrill when he could finally bring one of his fantasies to life.

Chapter 36

The air was filled with the screaming of the skill saw. The sweet smell of sawdust swirled in the air, mingling with the smell of decay that hung heavy throughout the house.

Ferris stopped working momentarily to rest, arching his back to ease his muscles. He looked around and was pleased with the progress. It was coming along nicely. There were still a few areas that needed chain link fence installed, to prevent anyone from getting too close to the props.

He removed a handkerchief from his back pocket and wiped the sawdust from his face. This was the last of the flooring on the second floor that had to be replaced. He had installed rope lighting along the baseboards to help illuminate the walkway. Everything must meet insurance codes and the man should be here at the end of the month to check on his progress, which meant that he had to ensure his workroom was thoroughly cleaned.

He did a walk-through of the haunted house to see how everything looked. The prop that he'd made to greet the crowd reminded him of a Frankenstein figure. He stood over seven feet tall and was a combination of parts from several people. His torso came from one of the larger men; the legs came from two individuals, as did the feet, the same for the arms and hands. No two parts came from the same person. The eyes that would greet them glowed red. Even the skin was mismatched, and pieced together like a quilt. He'd lucked out and found the clothing at a thrift store up north. He didn't want new clothes for the creature. The pants were well worn and tattered. They were in a box marked rags.

The morgue was looking gruesome as well. The skin hung perfectly on the wall, giving it the appearance he wanted. Looking around though, he got an idea. Not only did he need the autopsy victim, but he needed a crazed doctor yielding a knife and looking over the crowd, and a nurse. He wanted the nurse to be a live prop. She would beg people to help her out of the room and yell that this guy was crazy. Of course the crowd would think it was the doctor she was referring to.

He contemplated adding a room of clowns, since most people were deathly afraid of them, but where would it go. It was difficult to make it fit into the theme. That may take some thinking.

He moved over to the taxidermy room to see if it needed anything. He observed it with a critical eye. One of the figures would make people do a double take. Standing in the center of the room was a woman that appeared to be a spider. This was one of his best creations yet, and it took some time to complete it. She had eight arms, four on each side, and what appeared to be bristles on her back. He'd used porcupines and carefully removed their fur with the quills attached. He then attached the fur to the woman's back, leaving areas of flesh showing. It was an unusual piece. He even arranged it so that she moved. The arms "walked" around the room. He was getting good at working with the pneumatics. This may be his best haunted house yet. There would be more animated props than in his previous haunted house attractions.

Overall, the room was quite remarkable. The grisly mismatched parts from humans and other animals in here made it impossible to simply walk past the room. Visitors would be shocked and appalled by what they saw.

In the far corner was another creature. Almost horse-like, standing on two feet. Its arms looked skinny, multi-jointed, and extremely long. He was considering whether he should add a werewolf creature to the room, but that depended on how much time he had.

Chapter 37

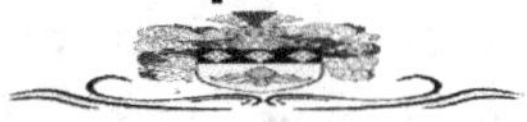

Allison Benoit joined Theresa Crawford and Janet Alden at the diner for ice cream. Those two girls had talked about the haunted house for the last two weeks. She was tired of hearing about it, and it was only August. It didn't open until October, and she knew they would want to go on opening day. She had to talk them out of it. She had no desire to step foot in that place.

Her two friends were talking about the blasted thing as soon as they entered the diner, "Come on, can't we talk about something else. Halloween is so lame. It is for losers."

"Aww, come on, this can be so much fun. A lot of the kids are talking about dressing up in costumes for opening day. It will be so cool. Nothing ever happens here on Halloween. We don't want to be the only ones who don't attend."

Allison was afraid she would have to admit defeat; maybe by the time Halloween was here everyone would be tired of talking about it and would lose interest. Allison shrugged her shoulders and took a spoonful of her ice cream, "I guess if y'all want something lame to do then we can go."

Theresa and Janet looked at each other and shrugged their shoulders. "Several of the kids have walked by it and they said it even looks creepy from the outside. They swear you can hear moans and screams coming from the house. One kid even tried to get in, but everything was locked up tight. And then Mr. Ferris caught him. I bet Trey peed in his pants when he was caught too. They said Mr. Ferris grabbed him by the collar and escorted him off the property. The man told him that if he caught anyone else on the property they would not be allowed there for opening day."

Allison wondered if she should test that theory, but the thought of sneaking over there gave her the creeps.

Chapter 38

An intense pain roared through Ray Broussard's head. Whatever his captor used to knock him out left him with the worst hangover he had ever experienced. He had been living on the streets of New Orleans for over twenty years and never once had to worry about being attacked. He had heard stories before from some of his partners in crime about being in the wrong area at the wrong time, but he heeded those warnings and had never had problems. As his vision adjusted to the darkness, he had a suspicion that he was in the trunk of a car.

Before he could think of a plan of attack, his captor opened the car trunk.

He asked, "Who are you? What are you planning on doing to me?"

Ferris laughed menacingly, "Relax old man. I have a special part cast just for you. When I saw you downtown, I knew I had to have you. You are perfect for the grave digger. If you want to survive, then you must do exactly what you are told to do."

Life could be harsh. Ray Broussard stared hard at his captor. He looked vaguely familiar, but his eyes were blank, vacant, as if he had no soul. He wished he could place where he had seen him before. Fear seeped from his pores now.

Chapter 39

Caitlyn stopped by Nemo's on the way home to pick up the lasagna and tiramisu she had ordered for supper. She remembered Gregory commenting on it, and decided it would be perfect for tonight. She had everything ready at the house for the green salad and even had a bottle of Chianti chilling. Although she wasn't sure it was as good as the one he ordered. She also stopped by the bakery and bought a fresh loaf of bread.

Once home, she had enough time to put everything in the oven to keep it warm while she took a quick shower. She couldn't wait for Gregory to arrive. Maybe with them eating at her house, she would have a chance to get closer to him. She hoped he stayed the night.

As she was getting dressed, she heard the doorbell ring. She called out, "Just a minute." She rushed to the door to let him in. She was surprised to find him holding a gorgeous bouquet of flowers in one arm and a box of chocolates in the other. "I wasn't sure what you had planned for supper, so I decided chocolate and flowers would go over better than wine."

She reached up and kissed him, "Chocolate and flowers are better than wine any day. I don't understand why a woman hasn't snatched you up before now."

"I'm just unlucky in love I guess, or maybe that is lucky."

She laughed, "Well, it is good luck on my part. Come on in. I have to confess that I cheated on supper. The only thing I

made is the green salad, and that came from a bag. The
lasagna and tiramisu came from Nemo's."

"Sounds perfect to me. It smells delicious."

She burst out laughing, "You are too much. I have a bottle
of Chianti chilling in the fridge if you want to open it. I'll fix
our plates. Would you prefer to dine al fresco or sit in the
dining room?"

Gregory looked over at her, "It's muggy outside if you want
to eat inside?"

"That sounds good to me." Caitlyn set their plates in the
dining room while Gregory opened the Chianti.

He called out, "Where is your corkscrew?"

"Oh, I'm sorry. I thought I had set it on the counter. It's
one of those new CO2 things. The guy at the wine shop told
me they were better than the old fashioned ones."

***

It was near the wine glasses. He didn't know how he'd
missed it. It wasn't like he didn't see them all the time.
He'd never thought of them when he opened a bottle of
wine, there were so many other things they were useful for.

"Okay, I found it. I was looking for an actual corkscrew."

He brought them each a glass of wine to the dinner table.

***

Over dinner they talked about everything they had achieved
during the day. Caitlyn didn't realize there was so much

that went into preparing a haunted house. She never thought about insurance, permits, and such. It was much more complicated than she had ever imagined. She always thought a couple of months before it opened, they did everything. It was an actual year round job.

They moved into the living room to finish the wine and enjoy their dessert. She had wanted this room to look romantic, so earlier she lit several candles around the room.

She sat down on the couch with her legs curled up underneath her. She had hoped Gregory would sit next to her, but he chose one of the wingback chairs.

The more they talked and were together, the more she believed she was falling for him. His eyes seemed to light up when he talked about his work. His voice became animated when he talked about the different things he still wanted to accomplish. She had never met anyone who loved their job as much as he did. He had such passion for it.

She could not stop looking at his arms and wondering what it would be like to be wrapped in them. Just thinking about kissing him made her blush with excitement. She had to force herself not to let her eyes travel further down his body.

She was so engrossed in her private thoughts about him that she didn't hear what he was saying, "I'm sorry my mind must have drifted off."

"I was just saying that it's getting late, and I know you have to work in the morning. I should get going. It's a long drive for me as well."

She tried to hide her disappointment that he couldn't stay longer.

Caitlyn followed him to the door. She noticed how close he was to her. It would be so easy to reach up and kiss him.

"Thanks again for dinner."

Caitlyn wondered if he could hear her heart beating wildly in her chest. "Thank you so much for coming. I enjoy your company. We will have to do this again."

He leaned down and kissed her. Caitlyn, not wanting the kiss to end, wrapped her arms around his neck and pulled him in closer. The kiss deepened. He pulled her closer to his body. She melted against him. His erection pressed into her. At least she knew he was attracted to her. The man must have amazing willpower.

***

Gregory battled with his conscience. He shouldn't get involved with her. He still had a lot to do, but it felt so right being with her. The longer they kissed though, the harder it would be for him to walk away tonight.

"I better let you get to bed before this goes any further."

***

She wanted to tell him that he could stay, but she found it difficult to find her voice. She couldn't take the humiliation of rejection if he said no. Her body trembled with desire for him.

Gregory stepped out the door and walked to his car. Caitlyn watched as he drove away and waited until she no longer saw his taillights before she closed the door. She had hoped that he would change his mind, drive back, and take her straight to her bedroom. She realized that wasn't going to happen and locked the door. She felt cold from where his body had been

Her body ached for him. It would be a long night. She had never had a guy be the one to keep things from moving too fast. Was he too good to be true?

Chapter 40

Andi Johnson pulled on her red bustier and adjusted her leather skirt, making sure to hike it up higher. The red bustier was her favorite, it showed off her cleavage the best. She looked in the mirror and gave herself a seductive little smile.

She may not have looks going for her, but at least she had a fantastic body. She tried one more time to do something with the frizzy mess of hair on top of her head, but it was useless. Besides, once she walked out in the humid air, it would go right back to the way it was now. The guys may not look at her face twice, but her boobs caught their attention. It was the one thing that God gave her that she was proud of. She figured he gave her gigantic boobs to make up for the face she was born with.

Tonight she needed all the help she could get. She had heard through the grapevine that Angel was working the streets again. Angel had tried to go straight, but something must have happened, so now she was back. That meant Andi had to work twice as hard to get men. Angel was not only built, but she had a face men fell for.

***

After leaving Caitlyn's house he was too keyed up to go home. Besides, he may as well see if he could find someone to fit in with the haunted house. Opening day would be here before he knew it and there was still so much to do. Maybe he should wait and pursue a relationship with Caitlyn after Halloween. If he explained to her the importance of this grand opening she would understand why he had to hold off on a relationship. If he promised her a personal tour for the grand opening, then she may forgive him for paying more attention to the haunted house than her. Especially once she saw it firsthand.

Only he didn't know if he could stay away from her. She was like a drug that had made it into his blood stream. He found it more difficult to think about work. His mind kept drifting back to her.

He sat in his car, cloaked in the darkness, and gazed into the night waiting for a subject. He saw her walking his way.

As she neared the car he stepped out. She was so engrossed in her thoughts that she never heard him approach her. He wrapped one arm around her while the other held the ether soaked rag over her mouth and nose. She was out in no time. He looked around to make sure no one was watching and loaded her in the trunk.

Once home, he prepared his work station. He heard her waking up. Her breathing was still shallow. For a while he worried he had given her too high of a dosage of the drug, especially since he had no idea what drugs she'd taken beforehand. If she had died from the sedative, he would have had to change his plans on which prop he would create, but since she was still alive he could stick with his original plans.

***

Andi felt as if her head was about to explode and her stomach was churning. She wished she could remember what had happened.

Her eyelids were heavy; she couldn't seem to open them. She licked her dry lips and forced her eyes open. Panic burned through the chaos in her head. Where was she? Fear constricted in her throat. She tried to force it back. A cold sweat broke out across her body.

She waited for her vision to adjust. Terror coursed through her veins. She needed to remain calm and figure out where she was. Complete horror gripped her as she realized she was restrained to a table of some kind. She had found herself in some dire situations before, but nothing like this. Her apprehension grew.

She watched in horror as he positioned a stool in front of her and pulled out his sharpening stone and knife. Her eyes were wide with fear as she noticed each pass the blade made along the stone. Once he finished, he ran it along the skin of his arm and watched as it shaved off a fine layer of hair. A smile of satisfaction formed across his face. "Perfect don't you think? It should be sharp enough now."

"For what?" Her eyes glistened with fresh tears.

He rose to his feet to move the stool. "I'm still wondering which scene you will fit in best. There are so many possibilities."

What did this man have planned? What did he mean by scene? Her mind raced with images of the vicious, vile things he could do to her. She struggled against the restraints. She had to get out of here. A dozen promises and pleas for forgiveness of sins ran off her lips as she begged God to free her. She vowed to change her ways, go on the straight and narrow if she lived. She prayed with all of her heart .

White-hot pain tore through her as he carved into her body with the knife. There was so much blood. It seemed to be everywhere she looked. She had lost count of the number of the times he'd stabbed and cut her.

***

He heard the pitiful whimpering coming from her. Having completed the look he needed he decided to put her out of her misery so that he could prepare the prop for the final stages. He picked up the CO_2 cartridge and inserted it into her neck. He cut her one last time as the needle pierced her pale skin. He saw the life leave her body as the look of horror was frozen onto her face.

Chapter 41

Robert Arnold looked at the flyer one more time. They were being passed around town like candy. George kept bugging him, "Come on man, we have to go to this. I bet there will be girls crawling all over the place needing a strong man to hold onto."

Robert wasn't sure about this, "It's all hype. This will probably be lame."

"I don't know, everyone is talking about it dude. This guy already has one that is huge, and they say it scares the shit out of everyone."

Robert told him, "I don't know. It's a two hour drive to get there."

"Come on, I'll pay for the gas. You just have to drive. Who knows, we may even get lucky while we are there. We can probably get some more people to ride with us . Make a day of it. Besides, we don't want to be the only ones that don't go, and miss out on all the action," George stated enthusiastically. "Besides, this guy is supposed to give a new meaning to horror. I've been doing research on his creations. He is a master at designing haunted houses. It even comes with a warning about pregnant women and people with heart problems not going in. How cool would it be if while we were there someone had a heart attack or died from being scared to death?"

Robert held up his arms in surrender, "All right, all right! I'll go, but don't forget that you are paying for the gas. I can carry two more people in my car, but if we find some chicks down there, we won't be able to drive them anywhere, if you get my drift."

George nodded in agreement, "That's cool dude. This will be a night you won't forget. Man, I can't wait for October 1st to get here."

Chapter 42

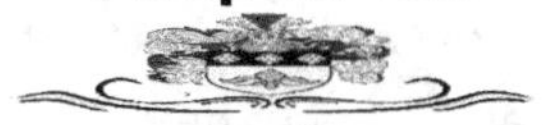

A few minutes past two o'clock in the morning a crash of thunder shook the plantation. Heavy, pounding rain began falling. The abruptness and the ferocity of the downpour had the same urgency of the perilous storm raging inside of him. He decided to wait until the grand opening of the haunted house before pursuing his relationship with Caitlyn. She seemed to take the news well, but he feared he may have ended that relationship before it got started.

Gregory continued working on the haunted house, knowing that he wouldn't be able to sleep. In his strive for success, sleepless nights were a constant for him.

He picked up a hammer to complete the finishing touches on the room. The material of the cotton t-shirt stretched across his biceps. The one good thing about manual labor was that it built up his muscles better than the gym. The need to finish pushed him forward.

***

Lying in bed Caitlyn tossed and turned. She was restless even before the storm hit. She had been extremely fidgety since Gregory Ferris called to let her know that he wanted to wait to pursue a relationship until after the haunted house grand opening. She knew she should understand the importance of this, but she wondered if it would always be like this; that work was more important than her.

She listened to the torrents of rain pound outside as thoughts plagued her mind. Somehow, the rain helped her find comfort. Rain rarely fell at this time of the year, but it may be just the remedy she needed for her insomnia. She listened to the rain as it struck the roof and windows, but it was failing to lull her into a deep slumber. Her mind refused to stop thinking about Gregory Ferris. If only she could convince him that she could help him; that she wanted to be there by his side. Should she stop by the new haunted house and offer to help him, or would that only upset him? She stared at the ceiling of her bedroom, brooding about what might have been, yearning to be in Gregory's arms.

Chapter 43

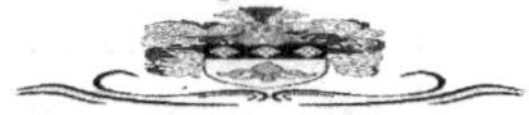

Unable to keep his mind off Caitlyn, and how desperate he was to see her, he decided to ignore the reasoning in his mind and headed out into the night to find another prop. Maybe that would help take his mind off her.

The sky loomed above, heavy with the promise of rain once again. As he drove to downtown New Orleans, the sky opened up. A steady stream of rain glistened in the night air. Countless droplets fell and glittered in the glare of the street lights.

***

Blake Sawyer stood under a bus stop, knowing that a bus didn't run at this hour. His fingers hugged the remains of a cigarette. He sucked on the filter with desperation, wishing he had something to eat. He couldn't believe his luck in finding a barely smoked cigarette. He wanted to savor it for as long as he could. His eyes darted through the rain, watching for signs of life. He saw a car fast approaching. He watched as it sped by, spraying water across his legs as it passed him.

He let out an exasperated sigh. Great, that's all he needed. He wasn't ready to call it a night. There had to be someone looking for some male companionship. He wondered how long he had been out here. He peered down the street, hoping to see some activity.

He heard another car approaching. He stood up, hoping that this may be a potential customer. The car seemed to stop down the road, maybe finding someone that had caught their fancy already. He slowly withdrew the cigarette from his lips and flicked the ashes off the end. He watched as the car eased his way. Maybe whoever was working that area didn't catch the person's interest. Blake struck a provocative pose, hoping to attract the driver's attention.

The car eased up to him. A large man was driving, and Blake noticed that he was incredibly sexy. He dropped the cigarette onto the ground and with the toe of his shoe ground it down to mush on the concrete. The faint scent of tobacco smoke still lingered.

He cleared his throat, waiting for the man to roll down his window. The attractive man gave him a flutter of anticipation in the pit of his stomach. He was going to be in for a treat tonight. He watched as the window slowly made its way down. "Is there something I can help you with?"

Gregory Ferris looked over the man one more time, "I hope so. Why don't you get in and we can discuss what you can do to help me?"

He unlocked the car door. Before opening the door, Blake asked, "You aren't a cop are you?"

Gregory chuckled, "No, I'm not a cop; I just have something special in store for you tonight."

As he got in, he asked the man, "What's your name?"

The stranger gave him a smile, "Names aren't important, are they?"

Looking out the windshield at the rain, "No, they aren't. So what are you looking for?" he asked.

Suddenly he felt an electrical shock travel through his body.

A fierce pain woke Blake. He opened his eyes slowly and tried to focus in on exactly what had woken him. He was lying on a table with his arms and legs restrained. The restraints were too tight to pull himself free. What was going on? Where was he? Why had someone brought him here? What kind of atrocities did this person have planned?

***

As the young man's struggles become weaker, Gregory picked up the CO2 cartridge and injected him. Death came quick and merciful for him. He drained the body of blood and prepared it for the final process.

Chapter 44

The high pitched scream echoed throughout the old house. The scream broke through her senses, waking her. The ensuing silence pulsated with evil. An electric heaviness hung in the air.

She tried to hide in the shadows of the room. Her knees were too weak to stand. She was disoriented and had the worst taste in her mouth. She was ready for death.

Sara Madison stared out into the hallway with little thought and even less awareness about who had screamed. Time had stopped for her in this mysteriously evil place. There was no escape from here. She had tried on numerous occasions. The glass that he used for the door would not budge. Her shoulders hurt from the attempts. The windows had bars across them. Her palms were bloody and raw from the failed attempts at pulling them away from the window.

This place was a true hellhole. It was what nightmares were made of.

She raised her hand to the deep gash on her forehead to see if it had stopped bleeding. She'd thought she had found a way to escape, but that had proven to be a false hope.

On top of that, she had fallen and busted her head open. She must be weaker than she thought. Her captor fed her, but only enough to keep her alive.

She continuously wondered if this would be the day she died.

The only thing to do was sit and stare out the door. Occasionally he passed with a mannequin or some other item he was using. The hammering and sawing were incessant, plaguing her day and night. She wondered if this man was even human, he seemed to never sleep.

She sat against the wall, drawing her arms around her knees. If she had chosen a different life for herself, would she still be in this situation, or was this her fate? She couldn't remember the last time she'd had a joint. She could go for a hit of coke right now. The DT's had lessened, but she could use something to numb herself from this hell.

She never knew if what she saw was real or a hallucination. Whoever her captor was, he had yet to touch or harm her. He locked her in this room, and other than mealtime, he paid no attention to her. He'd mentioned something in the past about how privileged she was to be a part of this haunted house. She wondered if the man was higher than a kite.

The air constantly smelled of decay and something else that she couldn't place. Almost as if meat was rotting somewhere. It must be nearing daybreak, a tiny piece of light started shining through the window.

She tried to recall her life before the prostitution, the drugs, and winding up here. She had to have been happy once. She tried desperately to remember, but it came in bits and pieces. More than likely, all the drugs she'd taken over the last year had fried her mind. If she closed her eyes, she could almost picture her dog from when she was little. It was a Jack Russell, but she couldn't recall his name. In her mind, she could see him lying on her bed with her as she slept. Every now and then she could recall what her childhood home had looked like. Did her parents still live there? Did they think of her?

She could see her parents attending Sunday mass, begging her to come with them. She remembered letting them down, how she liked to party on Saturday nights. She saw herself happy and laughing, but that was a dream. She couldn't remember the last time she'd actually laughed.

She still could not remember how she'd gotten here. It was all a blur. What was she doing when the man captured her?

She was in such deep concentration; she almost didn't hear the voices. Was someone talking? She shouted out, "Help me. Please help me!"

No one answered. Maybe she'd just imagined she heard something.

This place gave her the creeps. It resembled a hospital room, but with a serious dark side. She had looked at the figures in here several times, and she still wasn't sure if they were real or fake. She kept waiting for one to reach out and grab her.

Her captor told her that she was supposed to be the crazed nurse begging to get out. He didn't have to worry about that. She wanted out, and she wanted out now.

Chapter 45

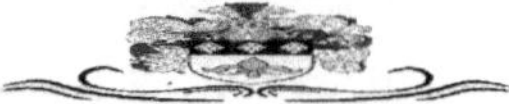

Caitlyn planned to leave work early this afternoon. She hadn't heard from Gregory Ferris since he told her that he needed to wait until after opening night before he could pursue a relationship. At first, she was going to blow off his invitation, but she hadn't been able to get him out of her mind.

On the drive home Caitlyn listened to the local news. Everyone was talking about the grand opening of Gregory's haunted house. With as much press as the grand opening was getting, it was sure to be a success.

She was anxious to get on the road and see Gregory tonight. She wondered if he would even have time to acknowledge that she was there.

Chapter 46

Shawn Granger and his friends decided to go check out Gregory Ferris's newest haunted house. He had tried to get in touch with Amy Guillory several times, but it was like she had dropped off the face of the earth. She had told him that they were through. She wanted a real man, whatever that meant. He had assumed she was just on the rag or something and would get over it, but he guessed he was wrong. She was ignoring him.

Shawn and his friends left New Orleans early so they could be in Point Creole for four o'clock. None of them wanted to wait in line long before checking out the haunted house. Shawn had a feeling that it would be a night that he would never forget.

After seeing the line of people when they arrived, he was glad they'd gotten here when they did. As it was, they would probably have to wait at least an hour before they could enter. They kicked back and waited in line. At least it wasn't hot. Shawn looked over the crowd, figuring he would see Amy and her friends here. This was the kind of thing they liked. He didn't know why he was so worried about whether or not he saw her. She dumped him; it was her loss.

As the sun went down, he heard Gregory Ferris thanking everyone for coming to the grand opening. Shawn couldn't wait to get inside. The setting from outside was sinister and he could imagine what it must be like inside.

As they entered the house, Shawn was amazed at the man's talent. He was wasting it by keeping his talent to himself. He could make a fortune selling these things online. As they moved through the house, Shawn felt his heart pound in his chest. The voodoo priestess gave him a start. The whole room was downright awesome. He would love to have an imagination like this man. They needed to go back through, in case he had missed anything. There were so many awesome details, and he didn't want to miss anything.

Suddenly, Shawn stopped dead in his tracks. A prop caught his attention and gave him a chill as he stared at it. Others tried to push him on, but he remained frozen in place. It couldn't be her! There was no way! This had to be a trick. He couldn't take his eyes off the prop. He looked around this house of horrors, taking in each scene carefully. Were these people begging to be freed prisoners? Or was this part of the show? There was no doubt in his mind that this prop was his girlfriend. What kind of sick bastard was this? He walked back to the autopsy room, against the flow of the crowd, and tried to get the nurse's attention. "Miss, miss over here. Please miss, I need to talk to you."

***

She couldn't believe one of these people wanted to talk to her. Could this man be her knight in shining armor?

"Are you trying to escape from this place? Please tell me this is some kind of act?"

She shook her head, "No! Please, you have to help me get out of here. He is keeping us captive. I think some of these people may have been killed. I don't think these are actual mannequins."

Shawn's blood ran cold. That was what he feared. He pulled out his phone and called nine-one-one. He hoped the operator believed him and didn't think it was a prank call. He told the young girl, "You may have to scream at the operator to get her to believe you, okay? I will hold the phone up to the glass." Shawn prayed that the person who did this didn't notice what was going on. If he did, then there was a chance that he would become part of this house of horrors.

He heard the operator pick up, "Please you have to believe me. I am in Point Creole at the new haunted house. A young girl here swears she is being held prisoner. I believe there are more people being held as well. Also, my girlfriend who has been missing is here, but I think she's dead already. She isn't moving. You have to help us."

"Sir this is for serious emergencies only. You can be arrested for making prank calls."

"Miss I know that, but listen to the girl, she is begging for help."

Shawn put the phone up to the glass, hoping the operator could hear the young girl, "Please listen to him. You have to get us out of here. I don't want to die."

The operator wasn't sure whether to believe the young man and girl on the phone. This could all be a prank, but if it wasn't, and she didn't act on this call, it would cost her this job. She would rather send a deputy out to check things out just to make sure.

"Sir, I will send a deputy your way. Please act natural and do not let anyone know that you have called the police." Shawn had no problem with that.

He told the young girl, "The police are on their way, but they want us to act like nothing happened, okay? Can you do that?"

She shook her head and prayed that the police hurried. She was ready to get out of here.

Chapter 47

It was the big night of the grand opening of the haunted house and Allison Benoit was scared to death. They were supposed to dress up as zombies and meet at Theresa's house. Theresa would drive them over there, but Allison prayed that her friends backed out. She didn't think she could go through with this. She wasn't even there yet and her hands were already cold and clammy from fear.

By the time Allison made it to Theresa's house, Janet Alden was there and both girls were waiting outside for her. "Hurry up Allison! I want to get there so we don't have to wait in line long. This is so exciting. It will be awesome."

When they arrived at the plantation, the line had to be a mile long already. This was going to be pure torture for Allison, but at least she had to wait a while before she had to go in. From here, she could hear the screams as people went through the haunted house. Her heart was ready to beat out of her chest. She swore she would throw up right here.

The windows were no longer boarded up, and they were flashing various colors; a mixture of whites, purples, and maybe orange. The screams were loud enough to wake the dead. As they stepped closer, Allison swore the ground was shaking underneath them. As the wind picked up, the trees shook and a low howl blew through the area. Allison jumped when she saw a shadow pass in front of one of the upstairs windows. She was scared out of her mind and they were still in the parking lot. How was she going to survive going inside? She tried to calm herself and not let her fears take control.

The line was moving faster than she'd anticipated. From where they stood, Allison saw the double doors that were the entrance to her personal hell. When they made it up the stairs, she caught a glimpse of the inside and shuddered in fear. Not only did it look dusty, as if nothing had been cleaned in decades, but she swore she saw heads staked onto the stairs. The place gave her the creeps. Theresa and Janet had not shut up since they'd left Theresa's house. Allison tried to get out of this one more time, "It's not too late to change our minds."

Janet looked at her, "Are you crazy? This is so frickin' cool."

Standing on the porch Allison swore it got colder. Allison stated, "Listen; from here you can hear someone wailing. Are you sure this will be okay?"

Theresa let out a sigh, "You are such a chicken. It will be fine. This is all make believe anyway. Just some really expensive props that have been arranged to scare the hell out of us, that is all."

Allison hoped she was right. "If you say so."

Allison grabbed Janet's hand as they stepped inside. "So far it doesn't look so bad. It doesn't even look that scary from here."

Allison just looked at her, "Yeah, right," she thought to herself. She didn't think Theresa believed that statement either. She looked as white as a ghost.

As soon as the entrance doors closed, they were engulfed in darkness. Allison screamed bloody murder and tried to push her way back through the doors. She wanted out of here. She couldn't go through with this. Let them call her a chicken. Before she could go outside, police officers barged in the front door, telling them they had to leave. Allison wasn't sure what was going on, but they didn't have to tell her twice. She was more than happy to leave.

The crowd was riled up now. Police officers were trying to cordon off the crowd, making way for the paramedics. Chaos escalated as police and paramedics tried to push their way through the droves of people. The crime scene techs were trying to set up lights so that they could see what they were gathering.

All of a sudden, blinding lights flooded the area announcing that the local news crews had arrived. The camera operator tried to catch the moment as people rushed out of the haunted house and the police made their way in.

The crackle of the police radio broke through the maddening noise. A police officer was barking orders out left and right. "We need more help. Get the paramedics in here. We need something to break this glass. There are people trapped in the rooms, begging to get out."

A paramedic responded to the demands, "It will be at least half an hour before we can get more ambulances here, but they are on the way. We will set up a mobile medical clinic so we can treat injuries on site."

"We need to get them here as fast as possible. It's a mad house in there. There is no telling who is dead and who is alive without checking pulses on each body. There is so much blood."

EMT's were bringing people out and setting them up in the staging area. Another paramedic was checking them out and triaging them according to the severity of their injuries.

The double doors to the plantation became a revolving door of carnage.

One man was brought out on a stretcher in a full-blown seizure. His body arched and strained against the restraints. Another paramedic was sprawled on top of him trying to keep him on the gurney. There was no telling if he was being held prisoner or was a paying customer. The gore was more than some of the customers could handle and several people were complaining of chest pain. This was a true nightmare.

Another officer asked one of the paramedics, "Do you know how many more injured there are inside?"

The paramedic shook his head, "There is so much carnage in there. It's hard to tell. Did you get the person responsible for this?"

"Oh yeah, he was here for opening night. I don't think he knew what was happening. He never had a chance to run. A young man called from inside. I think he was frozen in fear when he saw his friend staring back at him."

Chapter 48

Sheriff Brett Savoie surveyed the crime scene and was surprised at the sheer number of news vans. It didn't take long for word to spread about what happened.

He never suspected that this haunted house was in reality a house of horrors. When he walked into the house, he knew that he wouldn't have a good night's sleep for a long time. The smell of blood and decay was rancid and thick in the air.

He couldn't believe there were survivors. He forced the bile down in his throat.

He could still feel the terror that resonated from the poor souls killed here. There was something eerie about a place where complete carnage was recently unleashed. Even the most hardened law enforcement personnel became subdued when around such violent deaths.

The stench wafted onto the porch. He could only imagine the horrors that had taken place in this house over the last year. What kind of person did this to another human being? The smell of blood and feces mixed with the overpowering smell of decaying bodies would forever be in his nostrils. No amount of vapor rub would vanquish the smell.

Once inside the plantation, the sheer scope of the crimes committed here hit him. He studied the props that were in actuality victims. Would they be able to identify these poor people? How many of these props were real human beings and how many were fake?

Forensics techs had been through the haunted house. The medical examiner stated that he would have a hard time determining the time of death. The victims found alive weren't certain how long they had been here, but one recalled it being right around Christmas when he was abducted.

Sheriff Savoie envisioned what this place would look like over the next few days. He doubted they would be able to remove the spilled blood from here.

The ghastly bodies were being removed. Dozens and dozens of evidence bags were being collected. Dried blood coated the walls and floors. As a haunted house, it would frighten everyone that passed through its doors. Sheriff Savoie didn't understand why Ferris went to this extreme. The man had a real talent and could have put that talent to good use. The other haunted house was being dissected as well. So far, it appeared to be a mirror image of this one.

If only these walls could talk and tell them what horrors they'd witnessed. Being careful of where he stepped, he moved deeper into the house. He approached one room where a woman was nailed to the floor as if she was a bear skin rug. Repulsion for what she must have gone through raged through his body.

In another room there was a naked woman hanging upside down. She had been deboned and disemboweled.

The forensic techs found a refrigerator of blood along with freezers full of miscellaneous body parts.

The once beautiful antique furniture had been ruined from all the blood and cobwebs. What possessed a man to do this?

He heard one of the detectives swear and went to see what was wrong. "Sir, we need to get Department of Wildlife and Fisheries down here A.S.A.P. There are hundreds of snakes in a room with a woman. I think she's dead because she is just standing there. They are slithering all around her, sir."

Sheriff Savoie went upstairs to see if the young man was exaggerating and his skin crawled as he watched the snakes slither around the room. This man could have been considered a pure genius. A lot of detail went into each of the scenes. Everything was in such detail that you couldn't help but be impressed, if it weren't for all of the mutilated bodies. Looking at each room, you felt as if the horror was playing out right before your eyes.

Chapter 49

Caitlyn Reed watched in horror as the police arrived and arrested Gregory Ferris. She wasn't sure what happened. She went in search of Thomas and Grace Billiot. Maybe they would have some answers.

She kept hearing various rumors from the crowd, but surely those rumors couldn't be right. Why would Gregory have used real humans for his projects? He wasn't that demented was he?

***

Gregory Ferris didn't understand how someone discovered that the props were real people. This was the first time someone suspected anything of the sort. The locals wondered what kind of hell on earth had been unleashed onto this once peaceful town. The public was outraged that he had made money on these people's deaths.

No one understood that this was art. Of course, most people were narrow-minded and did not see the true genius behind his work. It took skill to kill someone at just the right moment in time.

Channel 9 in New Orleans was the first to air the story. After observing the reporter, Gregory realized the only reason she was hired was because of her boobs. When gravity set in, she would have massive backaches. She smiled and talked into the microphone, but could not look at his pride and joy. Occasionally she might glance at the crime scene tape. It was as if she was afraid to look at the house. Yes, this was his best attraction yet, and thanks to an unknown citizen, the world would never get to enjoy it.

When the plantation was a haunted house it was the scariest thing people had ever seen, but now that the truth was out the reviews had changed. Now, it was the most horrifying thing anyone had ever seen. How easily people's minds could be swayed. Why couldn't they understand his genius? Did they not realize that this was a piece of spectacular art? This was truly a *haunted house.*

www.ingramcontent.com/pod-product-compliance
Lightning Source LLC
Chambersburg PA
CBHW071825190726
48292CB00005B/1613